SOLE POSSESSION

Gillian Baxter

Copyright © 2020 Gillian Baxter

All rights reserved

The characters and events portrayed in this book are fictitious. Any similarity to real persons, living or dead, is coincidental and not intended by the author.

No part of this book may be reproduced, or stored in a retrieval system, or transmitted in any form or by any means, electronic, mechanical, photocopying, recording, or otherwise, without express written permission of the author. The only exception is by a reviewer, who may quote short excerpts in a review.

Printed in the United Kingdom

First printing: September 2020

CONTENTS

Title Page	1
Copyright	2
Prologue.	7
Chapter one.	10
Chapter two.	26
Chapter three.	41
Chapter four.	53
Chapter five.	54
Chapter six.	58
Chapter seven.	61
Chapter eight.	75
Chapter nine.	77
Chapter ten.	88
Chapter eleven.	97
Chapter twelve.	107
Chapter thirteen.	109
Chapter fourteen.	120

Chapter fifteen.	122
Chapter sixteen.	126
Chapter seventeen.	128
Chapter eighteen.	135
Chapter nineteen.	142
Chapter twenty.	153
Chapter twenty one	167
Chapter twenty two	187
Chapter twenty three.	199

Preseli Seasons

Winter.

Rain in grey columns like tall ghosts walking
Between the farmlands and the barren hills.
Grey rocks, grey water, grey skies, grey birds
Tossed low and crying where the wide marsh fills.

The past is in the rain, and long years to come
Veiled and hidden by time
The wind blows on and the clouds hang low
And the ghosts drift by in line.

Spring.

A light that shines and shimmers and moves
Over hills that might scarcely be there.
The sheep are back and the skylarks soar
Their song shimmers down through the air.

The ghosts are gone, it's the fairies turn
In the magical changing light.
There are other worlds not a breath away
Through the mists that touch on the heights.

Summer

The streams shrink down and the flickering fish
Lie low as the herons hunt.
In the wavering heat the bluestones move
And the bracken parts in front.

On midsummer's night the old gods stir
As the moonlight silvers the moor.

GILLIAN BAXTER

The owl flies low and his hunting cry
Springs open the cromleck's door.

Autumn.

Purple and gold are the moorlands now,
Brown and purple and gold,
The streams fill up as the storms roar in
And the sheep go down to the fold.

The year turns on with the cooling days,
The hills are shrunken and old.
From the ancient rocks the mist rolls down
And the ghosts come back with the cold.

PROLOGUE.

'It's no good, it'll have to go.'
The blond woman in the smart designer jacket and black trousers was tapping her feet impatiently.
'I'm not paying for any more vets or your livery fees while my daughter's in a coma all due to this animal.'
The animal in question, a once nice-looking bay pony with a breedy head and a white patch on his neck and one on his hind quarters, stood with drooping head in the yard. It had been trace clipped but the clip was growing out now, in March, and it had obviously recently lost weight. There were the scabby remains of old cuts on its legs and its eyes looked dull and withdrawn.
'You mean the knacker?' Marg, the middle-aged woman holding the rope had a short, no-nonsense haircut and yard clothes. 'Are you sure? Sylva is so fond of him and Simon reckons she dreams about him.'
'How does he know she dreams about anything?' The woman looked despairing. 'She just gabbles away; the hospital say it's just a reflex. Just get rid of it, I don't care how, it's proved dangerous.'
She turned to walk away to her smart car and Marg

sighed. Spotlight had always been difficult with anyone except his owner, withdrawn and different Sylva, who had found him in a sale, neglected and terrified of everything, with scars from vicious treatment on his head and flank. She had persuaded her brother to buy him for her and they had formed a tremendous bond, the frightened pony and the fragile girl, but there was no proof that he was dangerous, no one knew what had happened on the day he had come home alone with cuts on his legs and his rider had been found unconscious in the road. Slip marks had shown that he had bolted and later fallen but there had been no witnesses. The pony had been hard to catch that day, running round the yard and back to the gate almost as if he wanted someone to follow him. It had occurred to her afterwards that it was as though he knew Sylva needed help, but she had decided that it was too imaginative.

She had done her best for him up to now although the cuts had been slow to heal and it had been hard to keep any condition on him since the accident. If he had been a dog she would have thought that he was pining for his owner but she did not believe that horses formed that strong an attachment for a human. She couldn't have him put down, though, she decided. That could be the end for odd, withdrawn Sylva if she ever woke up again and found out, and Simon, her twin, would be devastated on her behalf. There must be another way. She would ask around.

Two weeks later.

The pony stood just inside the gate. Behind him the latch clattered and grated and footsteps squelched away. A door opened and closed, an engine chugged into life, and the sound of it moved away to the road. There was a great stillness, and a feeling of space, and suddenly, hopefully, he whinnied. There was no reply, and as the dusk thickened he knew that he was quite alone. It felt utterly strange after the small paddocks and enclosed spaces that he was used to with the distant hum of traffic, the company of other horses, and the feel and scent of the human who had
been his security. Suddenly he was afraid, afraid to move forward into this strange place of
unfamiliar smells and half-seen shapes where even the grass under his feet smelled strange. He would wait, she would come, she always had before.

CHAPTER ONE.

Spring was coming, the high moorland of West Wales was still brown but the low sheep fields were turning green and there were green buds on the thorn bushes. There were patches of flaming gold flowers on the gorse and there were tadpoles in the still patches of water beside the track. There was some slight warmth in the sun, and the light was dazzling in the clear, bright air. Patsy stopped her horse at the point where the track turned along the hillside and Goliath was happy to stop, blown after cantering all the way up from the flat land below them. He was a skewbald cob, not Welsh but what was called traditional, stocky and strong and still lively to ride in spite of his eighteen years.
Patsy was not young herself, sixty five, a bit stiff in the joints but still active. Her hair was still mainly dark with only a touch of grey and there was a youthful look about her. She was English but after five years she felt settled in her life in this fairly sparsely occupied country. She asked Golly to walk on and they followed the track as it turned steeply downhill back towards the sheep fields and the gate back to the road. There was a herd of moor ponies lower down, graz-

ing on the emerging patches of green, several with foals beside them, and Golly pricked his ears towards them. They were pretty little animals, purebred Welsh Mountain ponies owned by a local farmer whose youngsters, with famous blood lines, were in demand by breeders all over the world. Seeing Golly approaching they began to move away and Patsy noticed a stranger, a bigger pony than the Section A's, a bay with longer legs and a look of breeding in his head. He was thin, his coat rough, and as he began to follow the others the showy and possessive grey stallion ran at him.

'Dumped,' thought Patsy at once. It happened sometimes with people finding, too late, how much ponies cost to keep and how hard it could be to find buyers for them. Too sentimental to have them put down instead they turned unsuitable animals out to fend for themselves, not realising how hard and sometimes extreme conditions could be out on these wild, rough hills.

The bay pony swung away from the attack and, seeing Golly, it started hesitantly towards him and Patsy saw that it was lame. She stopped to wait until it was a few strides away, ears pricked, and Golly wickered a greeting. The pony came closer, stretching out its nose, and Golly cheerfully reached his nose to nuzzle it.

'Hello,' said Patsy. 'Who are you, I wonder.'

The pony had been trace-clipped earlier in the year, Patsy could see the line between the rough winter coat and the new growth, but there were scabby old cuts on its legs and it looked thin and poor. There was a small patch of white halfway up its neck leading to a white lock of mane and a small white patch on its quarters but otherwise it looked whole coloured.

"I'll have to come back, with Katy and a head collar, and see if we can catch it," she decided. Katy was her daughter, married to the son of Patsy's neighbouring farmer. For now all she could do was tell Golly to walk on and head for home.

The pony followed a few steps behind until Patsy reached the gate off the moor and as she closed it and rode on he called to Golly, who swung his head to listen.

'I'll be back,' Patsy told him, wishing that he could understand, but there was no more that she could do for the moment.

Patsy could see that her daughter was not there as she let herself and Golly in through her gate beside the cattle grid into her yard. Her stone-built traditional farmhouse was in front of her and to the left two the old stone stables had been rebuilt as a cottage for Katy and Gareth and their Land Rover was missing. They would be at Gareth's family farm next door, helping with setting up pens for the lambing which was just beginning, and Patsy knew that the pony would have to be left for another day. Both Katy and Gareth worked from home most days, both involved in computer work for small offices and homes, but at busy times Gareth helped his parents. He had helped to build some new stables in a barn behind the house for Patsy and now she led Golly down to his box.

Out in the field Eithin Aur, the Welsh cob mare, whinnied a welcome and her son, Hedfa Aur,
 gave his welcoming stallion scream and came to his gate at his showy, high-stepping cob trot. He was a magnificent animal, supreme cob champion at the Royal Welsh show last year, a shining, big crested chestnut with a flaxen mane and tail, and he was starting to raise interest as a possible sire. Golly shared his field as companion and the two horses got on well together.

Patsy and Katy had broken his mother in, not without trouble as she had been a largely un-handled four year old before she had her son, and Katy now rode her. She shared her field next to her son with Osbourne, a big oddly marked piebald horse with a white body and black head and mane. Osbourne belonged to an English neighbour of theirs, Mack. He and his wife Tabitha, both a similar age to Patsy, were away on a world cruise, 'before we get quite into our dotage,' Mack, who showed no sign of that being soon, had told Patsy. Osbourne was therefore holidaying himself with the Bryn Uchaf horses.

Patsy missed her rides with Mack, he was cheerful, undemanding company and she would be glad when he returned. He had shown her the safe ways over the rough hills with their bogs and drops and changing weather, they had ridden together for hours and talked about everything under the sun. Mack was the writer of a very successful series of thrillers based on some semi-secret work that he had done, many years ago, in the foreign office and on the royalties of which he had been able to buy a house in his beloved West Wales. Patsy knew that Mack loved the hills but his sharp-tongued wife grew bored, which had led to this cruise.

Patsy unsaddled Golly and turned him back out with Hedfa Aur and stayed to watch, leaning on the gate, as the two horses moved away to graze. They were quite a contrast, the shining stallion with his crested neck and bold eye and the plainly marked gypsy cob with his hairy legs and solid, big boned frame, but to Patsy they were both irreplaceable.

'They're great boys, both of them,' she commented to the sparkling air, but as always now there was no reaction. There had been a time when Patsy thought that she shared Bryn Uchaf with the shade of its previous owner, the prickly, resentful Welsh farmer who had owned Eithin Aur's sire, Bryn Uchaf Highflyer, but the sense of another presence had now been long gone, although Patsy
sometimes missed it.

Her four pet sheep, orphaned and bottle fed lambs who had stayed on, were eyeing her, hopeful of tit bits, until she turned away to tidy the stable leaving the horses to their grass, sweet with the rise of spring. The cats came to meet her, hoping for lunch, and Patsy stroked the tortoise shell mother of the tribe. She had known Emrys when he was alive and never been really afraid of him, or what remained of him, afterwards.

By the time the jobs were done the morning sun had become veiled as thin cloud drifted into the hills from the sea and Patsy knew that it would rain later. She had eaten a sandwich for lunch and was spending half an hour with a book when she heard Katy and Gareth drive in and Katy called in to report that they were home. She put her head in to greet her mother, her curly blond hair damp already from the first drops of rain, and Patsy told her about the pony.

'I'll come out with you to check it tomorrow,' Katy promised. 'I've got a bit of work to catch up on this afternoon.'

She went away down the yard to the cottage and Patsy checked on Facebook to see if there was any mention of a missing pony. As she had expected there was nothing. If it was a stray someone would have been round checking all the local farms but it had definitely looked more abandoned than straying.

The wind got up later, making the front door bang as it roared in from the sea, and Katy and Gareth helped to bring in the horses as it promised to be a rough night. Gareth had built the new barn with inside stabling for the horses and there was good shelter from the weather. The moorland ponies would not be bothered, they were used to the wild storms that brought sheaves of rain driving across their hills. They had their sheltering spots among the gorse bushes and in the ravines where the streams ran and they never shed their thick coats until instinct told them that the spring had really come to stay. The bay pony would feel the weather, though, with his half grown out trace-clip and his look of finer breeding. Patsy hoped that he would find shelter with the wild ponies but she doubted if the stallion would let him.

It was still raining next morning but the wind had dropped a little and Katy said that she would go with Patsy to look for the pony. They saddled up, Golly resigned to the fact that he was about to be asked to face the weather and the mare, whom Katy called 'Goldie,' an English version of her Welsh name which meant 'Golden Gorse', swinging round restlessly.

Out in the yard the wind came down from the hills in a stronger gust and the horses turned their tails to it but once their riders were settled they consented to face it and Golly led the way out to the road.

The gate onto the moor was hard to open, the wind catching it, but Golly helped Patsy to cope and Goldie shot through while she held it. There was a sweep of rain coming towards them in a grey mist and neither horse wanted to face into it.

'We'll never find him in this,' Katy shouted, and Patsy said, 'There's that gorse thicket in the dip, he could be there.'

They crossed the intervening stretch of open ground with the horses walking sideways with their heads low and their ears flattened to keep the rain out. They knew from the sudden disturbance among the thick bushes that there were ponies sheltering there, and the grey stallion met them, on guard, his mares behind, but the bay pony was not there. Golly and Goldie were not keen to go back into the wind and Katy shouted against it, 'we'll have to leave it,' and Patsy knew that she was right. The pony could be anywhere on the thousands of acres of open moorland.

Both their horses were only too glad to make for home but a little later, when they were settled in their sheltered field and she and her daughter were drinking coffee by the Rayburn with the dozing cats, Patsy felt guilty. They could have searched further, she thought, unused to such weather the bay pony would suffer. First thing tomorrow, she vowed, as a gust of the freshly strengthening wind shook the window, she would go out prepared to make a proper search.

It was very early the next morning when something woke Patsy and the mother cat, also disturbed, thumped off her feet to the ground. There was a faint line of light round the curtain and as she sat up Patsy heard Golly whinny and knew that something had alerted him. She got rather stiffly out of bed and peered out. It was light enough for her to see the brown and white horse at his gate, staring into the distance. Patsy knew that she would have to investigate. Katy would not wake, she usually slept through storms and domestic dramas, and Patsy pulled on jeans and a sweater and went downstairs to let herself out into the still, sweet scented, slightly misty light of early morning.

There was nothing obvious wrong. The other horses were still asleep, the mare and her son lying down with their legs tucked under them and noses on the ground, Osbourne flat on his side. Only Golly was awake, and he greeted Patsy with a soft nicker.

'What is it?' Patsy asked her old horse and Golly snorted and nudged her. He was staring away again towards the hills and now Patsy heard it herself, a faint whinny, just a whisper in the still air. Not the moor ponies, she decided, they only called to each other before joining up again.

'All right, we'll go and see,' Patsy told him, and she opened the gate and slipped the head collar, left handy on a hook by the gate, over his ears. Ten minutes later they were on their way up the track to the nearest moor gate.

The hills looked deserted, still and patched with mist over the streams. Golly was looking to the right, towards the undulating ground which hid Bedd-yr-Afanc, the monster's grave. This was one of the Preseli landmarks, a small cromlech, a double line of inward leaning stones about two feet high enclosing a slight hump of sheep bitten turf. Its origin was hidden in aeons of time, only a legend remained. The monster, it was told, had lived in the stream which ran under the nearby village, now across the road. It had preyed on young maidens until the villagers trapped and killed it and buried it in its moorland grave, bringing peace to the area. It was a spot which the moorland ponies avoided and Patsy had always been conscious of a stillness about it, a stillness and a vague sense of old, hidden menace. It was not still now, however, there was something between the stones, something brown and moving, and Golly whinnied and carried Patsy towards it.

The bay pony seemed to be cast. He must have tried to find some shelter in a spot away from the threat from the other ponies, lain down and found, when he tried to get up, that he could not get his legs under him. He called to Golly as he approached and tried again to stand up but Patsy could see that he was very weak. The weather and the wilderness had been too much for him. She knew that she could not deal with this alone and pulled out her phone to call Katy.

It would take Katy on foot about half an hour to reach them. Patsy got off Golly and led him closer to the pony who made another attempt to get up and again dropped back. His legs seemed to be working but the room between the cromlech stones was too uneven to make it easy. Patsy wondered if he had been afraid to wander far and had found some security in still being in sight of the gate. He seemed a bit comforted by Goliath's presence and Patsy settled to wait. The patchy mist drifted over them and Patsy shivered, conscious of the other-worldly feel which was part of this wild and ancient country. Golly snorted, his white whiskers beaded with moisture, and somewhere above the mist a buzzard mewed.

It seemed a long time before Golly pricked his ears and the bay pony raised his head and looking round Patsy had a brief glimpse through the mist of her daughter hurrying towards them, her long blond hair drifted across her face by the slight breeze which was starting to stir the mist. The pony saw her too; he whinnied, shrill and clear, and with a huge effort he stood up. His legs were shaking but as Katy emerged from the mist he took an unsteady step towards her, his head high and ears pricked, before he appeared to deflate. His ears went back and his head down in what looked like obvious disappointment and Patsy reached out to slap his side to persuade him to stay on his feet.

Katy had brought a head collar and a bucket containing pony nuts, and the pony let her put the head collar onto him. He sniffed at the food and took a doubtful mouthful and Katy scratched his neck under the ragged mane.

'Poor old boy,' she said. 'That was weird, it was almost as if he thought I was someone he knew.'

'I think he did.' Patsy stroked the thin, rough neck. 'That was why he managed to get up. See if he can follow Golly.'

It was slow going but gradually the pony loosened up and found a scrap of strength and at last they were off the moor and making their way past the cattle grid into the yard of Bryn Uchaf. The other horses greeted the sound and scent of a stranger with an assortment of calls but the pony ignored them. Katy led him into one of the spare boxes in the barn and Patsy put Golly into his stable and fetched a sheaf of hay for the pony while Katy shook wood chips out to make a bed. Slightly recovered by the shelter the pony nibbled at the hay and suddenly regained his appetite and began to eat voraciously. Katy fetched a bucket of water and she and Patsy leaned on his door to watch.

'I wonder if we'll ever find who owned him,' said Katy, and Patsy shrugged.

'I doubt it,' she said. 'He's obviously been in some sort of accident, perhaps the owner thought it would be too much trouble to get him right.'

'He isn't the usual dumped sort, though,' Katy was looking at the pony's nice conformation. 'How could anyone be so thoughtless?'

'People don't realise how rough it can be out there,' said Patsy. 'They see a stretch of open land and ponies grazing it and they don't realise how different those hardly little Welshies are.'

'I suppose,' Katy turned away. 'I'll see if Gareth has any ideas.'

She went to tell Gareth what had happened and he came to look, tidy for work in a blue sweater and dark trousers. He was a nice looking young man with a usually cheerful face and thick dark hair. He and Katy had been together for four years now, and although it had been a fairly stormy relationship they had stuck together and had got married just a year ago after deciding that it was time to start a family. That had not yet happened and Patsy suspected that Katy was almost relieved but Patsy was looking forward to grandchildren when it did.

'He looks a bit rough,' Gareth reached over the door to pat the pony, who stepped nervously back out of reach. 'I'll give Mum a ring and she'll ring around the locals and see if anyone knows anything, The laws dodgy about abandoned horses; they still belong to whoever dumped them, you could be said to have unlawfully moved him, and you would be responsible to his owner if anything happened to him.'

'I don't think there's much chance of an owner turning up,' said Patsy. 'But we couldn't have left him there.'

'What shall we do with him for now?' asked Katy.

'Leave him to settle,' advised Patsy. 'Golly can stay with him for a bit and If he seems alright later we could put him in the little paddock. I've got a feeling he might be here to stay. I'll tell the police but dumped ponies aren't exactly a priority.'

Katy and Gareth went off to their cottage and Patsy fed her friendly little flock of sheep and let her six bantams out into their large day time pen before going in for breakfast. She was followed by a tribe of cats complaining that the breakfast service was bad today. She poured dry food into their bowls and cereal into hers and settled down to eat at the gate legged table by the window.

This was her favourite room with its timber-beamed ceiling, the old green Rayburn chugging against the wall and the wooden staircase sloping up above. The window looked out over the fields to where her woods sloped away to the stream which ran around the edge of the property, and she could see her horses grazing and the resident pair of buzzards circling above as the last shreds of mist lifted.

Spring was almost here, Rhianne's holiday Pods, new venture last year, would soon be in demand by tourists and there had been talk of Patsy taking on a couple of safe cobs to provide mountain treks if there was a demand. It would give her a new venture and Katy would help.

She had never regretted the impulse that, at sixty, had made her buy this solid farmhouse and its land and move herself and her two old horses here from the overcrowded south east. Golly's long-time companion, little brown David with his mealy Exmoor nose, had left a sad gap when he died but her purchase of the in-foal cob mare had helped to heal that. She had sometimes been lonely although having Mack to ride with had helped and she had made friends around the district. Now that Katy was next door she no longer felt isolated.

By the end of the morning the bay pony seemed stronger. He had eaten all the hay that Patsy had given him and spent some time lying down with Golly companionably dozing in the next box. Patsy had telephoned the local police to report finding him and they accepted her report but said that there was little they could do. They repeated what Gareth had said about abandoned horses but assured her that reporting it to them would defuse any claim.

'It happens,' she was told. 'Get it checked for a microchip, although a lot still don't have one. It sounds as though someone just wanted to be rid of it,' and Patsy knew that it was true.

She checked his feet, which he accepted politely, and found one of the things wrong in a large stone jammed against the frog. Having looked the rest of him over she decided it was time to try turning him out.

She took Golly out first and put him into his field with the stallion who greeted him with a squeal and a display of acrobatics on his hind legs which the skewbald horse completely ignored. Hedfa Aur was becoming increasingly less peaceful as the covering season approached and Patsy was glad that she had

Gareth about to help handle him. It had been suggested that it might be sensible to send him to stand at stud at a professional cob yard but she knew, perhaps ridiculously, that the previous owner of her home would not approve. Emrys, who had owned his sire, Bryn Uchaf Highflyer, had been forced by financial reasons to sell Heddfa Aur's sire to a cob stud. That had ended badly when the stallion, fed on oats and stable kept for the breeding season, had managed to get out and break a leg. Emrys had never forgiven himself and, driven by debt and guilt, had shot himself and his dog in what was now Patsy's yard. She had not known this until she was living at Bryn Uchaf and had found that she was not entirely alone there.

The bay pony followed anxiously when she led him out. He was stiff but not noticeably lame now that the stone had gone, and when she unclipped the head collar rope and turned to let herself out of the gate he walked behind her as if anxious not to be left.

'It's all right,' Patsy told him. 'You aren't being deserted, go and have a look round.'

The pony seemed to understand. He turned back to survey the paddock, seeing the other horses in fields next door, and Hedfa Aur, seeing a stranger near his patch, challenged him with a masculine screech. The pony ignored him, he was gazing around, ears pricked, as if he was searching for something. Goldie wickered to him and Osbourne gave him a quick glance before going back to his grazing, but the pony did not seem interested. He began to circle his enclosure, following the fence round and still gazing into the distance in a way that Patsy was finding disturbing, and she left him to it while she went to tidy the stables that they had used. 'He's just confused,' she told herself. 'He'll settle.'

Miles away in a small whIte hospital room the girl in the white bed, connected to the monitor with its regular green light timing her responses, stirred and rolled her head on the pillow and murmured something. In the quiet Welsh field the pony suddenly whinnied and when there was no reply he finally moved away to start grazing.

CHAPTER TWO.

By teatime, when Patsy had eaten some lunch and done some necessary house work, the pony was grazing, although near to the gate rather than to the other horses. Katy, taking a break from her computer, called in wanting to discuss entering Hedfa Aur for the Cardigan Barley Saturday stallion show and parade which was drawing near. Barley Saturday was a local tradition, it had once been the occasion after sewing the spring barley at which cob stallions offered for stud were shown off. These days it had become a vintage vehicle display and general fete as well.

'He's going to be a handful this year,' Katy told her mother. 'But Gareth reckons he's up for it.'

'I wouldn't fancy it without him,' said Patsy. 'These cob stallions are a whole lot different to the thoroughbred types.'

'All fire and power, as they say,' Katy laughed. 'As some men try to be.'

'Including Gareth?' Patsy probed casually. She sometimes wondered about Katy's marriage, her daughter had been a bit wild herself once, and Gareth had always seemed to be quite a conventional choice for her although she knew that the partnership was sometimes stormy. Katy laughed again, although Patsy thought she sounded uneasy.

'He has his moments,' she said now, and Patsy realised how little she really understood her daughter or how committed her marriage really was. How would a baby, if there ever was one, affect her?

'You do want to show his lordship, don't you?' asked Katy now, and Patsy realised that her attention had wandered,

'Yes, of course, Barley Saturday is always a great occasion,' she said, and Katy put the entry form on the table.

'You'll do the entry then?' she asked, and Patsy promised that she would.

She went out as she always did to shut up the bantams and to check the horses before it got dark. The days were really lengthening now, the swallows were back, swooping in and out of the older buildings which were still there beside the new barn. The midges were out for them to feed on, also providing a great feed for the bats as they began to emerge into the dusk. The resident horses came to meet her for carrots and the bay pony joined in, coming quite eagerly to his gate.

Patsy handed out slices of carrot and then stayed, leaning on the gate, as they wandered back to the grass. It was very still now, and quiet. Somewhere in the wood a vixen screamed and a barn owl drifted low and unearthly across the field. The bay pony remained, again staring into the distance, and Patsy turned to look at him.

'What is it?' She asked him. 'Are you really waiting for someone? I wish you could tell me what happened. You look much too nice to have been dumped.'

The pony swung his head to look at her and then whinnied, listening for a reply, and when none came he finally turned away and started back across his field until the thickening dusk took him out of Patsy's sight.

"Would Emrys have been able to understand?" wondered Patsy, but she knew that Emrys was long gone.

Over the next few days the pony seemed to settle down. He was looking less poor, his flanks were less hollow and his summer coat was showing as the dead winter hair began to come out. Patsy brought him in and brushed him and once he accepted that she was not threatening he enjoyed it, leaning into the brush and pushing out his top lip with pleasure. With Barley Saturday drawing near Katy was in the next box working on Hedfa Aur's coat and his rich chestnut colouring was taking on its summer glow.

'He'll never look quite as perfect as the stallions that have been stabled,' said Katy, 'but I think he looks better, just not so artificially strung up.'

Patsy had heard about the 'cob boys' methods of keeping their stallions shut in boxes with closed top doors to make the most of their impressively fiery behaviour when they were brought out for viewing. It was one of the things that Emrys had blamed himself for when his Highflyer had been kept that way after he was forced to sell him. In any case his grandson was quite enough for Patsy to handle kept as he was with plenty of freedom.

Gareth's mother, Rhianne, had followed up her suggestion of finding some ponies for occasional treks.

'They belong to a friend of mine whose daughter used to ride' she explained. 'She's at Uni now and they need regular exercise to keep laminitis away. I said you might go and look. She loaned them out last summer, but the stable that had them isn't doing trekking anymore.'

'Have you had any of your visitors ask about treks?' Patsy asked her and Rhianne said that she had.

'The chance to ride would be another thing to attract visitors,' she said.' And our insurance company would add the risk to our policy.'

Patsy said that she would have a look at them the next week, after the show. She knew that with sheep prices down and little market for wool Gareth's mother could do with some extra income and it would be an enjoyable experience. It was a long time since the days when she used to help out escorting rides for a local riding school in her Surrey days.

Barley Saturday meant an early start. Judging took place first in a field just outside the town and the parade through the town centre followed, with all the exhibits as well as the vintage entries. Patsy's faithful old Transit horse box had been given a good wash down by Katy and Gareth had the job of leading the shining, excited stallion into it. Hedfa Aur was an experienced competitor and he knew what was coming. The bay pony watched over his gate as they loaded the stallion and as the ramp went up he whinnied, and

Patsy had a feeling that he had expected to go as well. They set off for Cardigan with Patsy driving and Katy and Gareth crammed in beside her.

Cardigan is a busy little market town beside the estuary of the River Teifi and today the main street was closed to traffic. Patsy took the back road and soon they were following other horse transport in through the gate. There were several trailers and some more impressive vehicles and a few horses had already been unloaded and were being walked about to settle them before their classes. They were not all cobs, there were classes for Welsh ponies, thoroughbreds, and heavy horses as well followed by a championship.

Hedfa Aur enjoyed shows. He bounced down from the lorry with Gareth holding firmly onto his head and greeted the other horses with a challenging shriek. There were several shrieks in reply and the stallion pranced round Gareth with head and tail high. He was well known to cob people after his great win at the Royal Welsh and several people congratulated Patsy on how well he looked.

'Old Emrys would be happy,' one of the older cob breeders told her. 'You've done him well girl.'

Patsy thanked him, knowing that it had taken some time for her to be greeted almost as an equal in spite of being English. It was Emrys's unseen influence and the horses that had earned her that.

There were some good cobs in Hedfa Aur's class, circling in the roughly trimmed grass ring in the middle of the field, but the shining little horse's blond mane and tail and spectacular action made him outstanding. He won his class for section D cobs and it was no real surprise when he went on to be show champion, beating the pretty white section A winner and the bigger horses.

'Will he be taking mares this season?' a lady who bred show ponies, asked Patsy.

'I hope so,' Patsy told her, and the lady, an efficient looking English lady, asked where he would be standing.

'At home,' Patsy knew that some of the breeders were doubtful about this, feeling that their mares would be better handled and safer at one of the professional studs, but she would not change her mind. The lady nodded and moved on and Patsy knew that she might have missed a possible client.

The main attraction of the day, the parade, was due to start at two o'clock. Patsy left Katy and Gareth to get the horse ready and walked down to the main street to find a good point from which to watch.

After a partly cloudy morning the sun had come out and the old Welsh town was bright with flags.

Patsy found herself a place on the outside of the slight curve in the road from which she would have the longest view, and the spectators stood pressed against the temporary barriers, chattering and expectant, children with ice creams and parents in summer frocks or shirt sleeves. In the distance, down the hill towards the old stone bridge across the Teifi estuary, there was the first clatter of hooves and a mounted marshal on a big hunter came into sight following a police car which was clearing the way.

There was an enthusiastic ripple of applause and after a moments pause the first horse appeared, the show champion, Hedfa Aur, all glowing coat and flashing trot, with Gareth running alongside with the reins long, letting the little stallion display his huge paces. Patsy felt a great rush of pride; in her lovely, home bred horse, her handsome son in law, and her feeling of being so much a part of this old festival with its far distant roots in this quiet, hidden part of an ancient country.

'Looking nice, aren't they,' said a quiet Welsh voice behind her, and Patsy looked round to see Rhianne, watching with her.

'Beautiful,' she replied. 'It's a good thing Gareth's fit, it's quite a climb up here.'

'He's always been a bit of a runner,' said Rhianne. 'Used to do the Ras Beca each year, usually got a finishing place.'

Patsy had watched the local fell race over part of the Preseli mountain range. It was rough, steep and often boggy going, no wonder Gareth could run with the stallion.

The rest of the parade was going by, the cobs and ponies, then the heavy horses, two donkeys, and then the horse drawn vehicles, traps and a trotting cart, a wedding carriage, a magnificent pair of Shire horses with a decorated hay cart, and a gypsy caravan drawn by a cheerful traditional cob, black and white, with full mane, tail, and feathers.

After the horses came the vintage farm vehicles, old tractors, an original harvester, and bringing up the rear in a roaring cloud of steam a traction engine. They were all enthusiastically cheered and money was willingly put into the collector's boxes. Patsy and Rhiannon smiled at each other.

'Always a great sight, that,' said Rhianne. 'Time we had ourselves a cup of tea. Call your girl and tell her I'll drop you home.'

Patsy realised that she could do with tea, her feet were sore from standing and it was quite hot now in the sun. She tapped in Katy's number and her daughter agreed that she and Gareth could happily deal with getting Hedfa Aur home.

There were several small cafes along the street and Patsy and Rhianne managed to find a space and settled with cups of tea and buttered Welsh cakes.

'Emrys would have been proud,' said Rhianne as she stirred her tea. 'His Highflyer was champion here you know.'

'No, I didn't know that,' Patsy realised that she might have guessed. Highflyer had been locally famous.

'Your boy is that like him,' Rhianne told her. 'I remember Emrys was over the moon, his cob from his little farm beating all the big boys. It was a real shame, things turning out for him like they did, but, fair play, it brought you and your Katy to us, and that made my Gareth happy.'

'And gave me the chance of a new life,' Patsy stirred her coffee. 'It's always hard to see how things will turn out but I've never regretted coming here.'

'I'm glad,' Rhianne reached across the table to pat her hand. 'It's done us well, it has, brought my boy back to settle near us, which he might never have done if he hadn't found good reason to with your girl. Be fine, now, if they make us both grandparents.'

Patsy agreed that it would, but she did wonder how Katy would feel if it really happened. She had always been restless and a bit insecure. How would being pregnant affect her?

They finished their tea and Patsy promised to go to see the trekking ponies next day. Outside the narrow pavements were still busy and Rhianne said 'Cardigan's festival day, I've always come since I was a child. Your friend Mack with the black and white horse will be sorry to miss It although his wife mocks our traditions a bit. Never really seemed to settle here somehow. Always liked to go somewhere else in the winters and now off on a cruise in the nicest part of our year.'

'Tabitha?' Patsy realised that she was right. Mack had come with them the previous year because Tabitha had not wanted to go. He had bought her ice cream and they had watched the parade together. She wondered how he was enjoying his cruise.

'Yes,' said Rhianne. 'Nice enough woman, but a sharp tongue on her. Not a bit like her husband. Good company for the riding is he?'

Patsy looked at her. Was Rhianne hinting at something or was she imagining it, but her friend was looking at her watch.

'Time we followed the young ones home,' she said. 'There's the sheep lambing and a couple of the first ones on the bottle. Well done today, I love watching your great little horse show himself off.'

She did not mention Mack again and Patsy decided that she was imagining things. Surely there wasn't really gossip about the time she spent riding with him?

The Transit was back by the time Rhianne dropped Patsy at home, and the stallion was in his stable, pulling hay from his net while Katy brushed sweat and dust from the outing off his gleaming coat.

Patsy saw that she was looking ruffled and she asked casually if the horse had travelled well.

'Horse was great,' Katy told her. 'My husband was the problem, moaning about my driving.'

'What had you done?' Patsy asked her and Katy shrugged, pushing her long hair off her hot face.

'Going too fast, apparently,' she said. 'As if he's the one who knows. He's only driven cows, falling about loose in a cattle trailer.'

Patsy suspected that Gareth could have been right, Katy had always been an impetuous driver, but she was not going to take sides. There would be some raised voices and tossing hair and then, Patsy knew of old, some lively making up. She changed the subject to talking about the horse and telling Katy about the stud inquiry.

'It's probably right you know,' Katy told her. 'If you really want him to make his name as a sire he'd get more mares at a recognised stud.'

Patsy laughed. 'Emrys would never forgive me,' she said. 'Anyway, I'm not really setting up as a stud, just a couple of mares coming to keep the line going in the

Highflyer name.'

Katy stared at her.

'You don't seriously mean you might offend a ghost?' she asked. 'Really Mum, I thought you'd forgotten all that, surely it was just because you were on your own here you got that idea about this place being haunted?'

'And don't you remember what happened when you and Gareth got up to no good in this house?' Patsy asked her, and Katy went red.

'Oh, that was just our guilty consciences imagining things,' she said. 'Anyway, this gold boy might do better with professionals, that's all, but if you want to struggle with covering here I expect Gareth will go on helping.'

She gave the stallion a pat and turned him to go out of the barn. Outside the bay pony was waiting at his gate and he greeted Hedfa Aur and Katy with a shrill whinny. Golly came to meet his friend and the stallion led the way off down the field at a trot but the pony stayed by his gate and when Katy went to him he sniffed her and then pushed his head under her arm and stood there without moving. Katy stroked him, looking sad, and Patsy said 'I think he's missing someone.'

'Someone who looks like me,' said Katy sadly. 'He seems to hope each time he sees me that I'm someone else, and when I'm not he sort of switches off.'

Patsy thought the same, but surely that person would not have abandoned him. Something must have happened to them.

The pony seemed to come back to acceptance. He stepped back, lifting his head, and turned away down his field to start grazing again.

The next day Patsy took Katy with her to look at the trekking ponies. Their owner, a rather flustered lady dressed in working out style of leggings and tank top, met them at the door of her sprawling modern bungalow. There were several cars parked outside and the sound of music came from inside.

'I'm Serena,' she said. 'I'm sorry, I forgot I'd got my yoga ladies at this time when I said when to come. Such a big veranda at the back, so much nicer than a hired room. The ponies are in the stable, would you mind looking without me? They've been borrowed for trekking before, no problems.'

Patsy said that it was fine.

She and Katy made their way round the end of the bungalow and down a path to a rough paddock with two wooden loose boxes in it. Two heads appeared at the sound of their steps and Katy fished some slices of carrot out of her pocket.

The ponies were a grey mare and a black gelding, both part-bred cobs. They both seemed friendly although the grey was more pushy and they were a useful height at about fourteen two.

'They look alright,' Katy was fending the grey off from pulling at her pocket. 'We could give them a try anyway. You could make a few pounds from it as well as Rhianne getting her extra attraction and it could be fun. I can arrange my work so that I can help.'

There was a musical chant coming from the house

and Serena, still looking flustered in spite of the yoga, told them that the ponies were called Cinders and Sweep.

'It will be such a relief not to have to worry about them,' she said. 'I've no time to exercise them and my horsey friends keep telling me they'll get laminitis. Rhianne said they'd be absolutely fine with you.'

They collected the ponies the following day. Driving home with them over the mountain Patsy surveyed the rough, steep country with its numerous hazards and hoped this trekking idea was not a mistake but she was committed now to trying it. After all, thanks to Mack's company she had learned her way about their home hills pretty well and she knew the safe, easy tracks. With normal luck not too much should go wrong.

Hedfa Aur was very interested when he saw the new arrivals but after prancing up and down his field as they were led past to their new field he realised that although one was a mare they were not for his attention and he calmed down. He had been full of himself after his trip out to Barley Saturday. When Patsy brought him in for his daily grooming he almost pulled her over and he was impatient in the stable, swinging about and pawing the ground. Katy was busy at home with a series of conference calls about the use of some new soft wear and Gareth had a day away working at his employer's central office in Cardiff. Patsy cut her grooming session short and the stallion towed her back to his field. Watching him prance away Patsy hoped that a few visiting mares would not make him more of a handful.

It was a relief to saddle peaceful Golly and go for a ride round the quiet lanes and bridle paths which lay behind her home. The fields were full of lambs and the banks were thick with primroses. Soon there would bluebells and their scent would fill the deep, high banked lanes. Patsy was sorry to think that Mack, who loved seeing the vibrant life come back to his much-loved hills, would miss this time of year. The wildflowers, growing scarce now in most of Britain, were one of the wonders of Pembrokeshire and Patsy knew that she would never tire of them.

Goliath ambled happily along as the light changed and a brisk, short-lived shower swept in from the west. This was another charm of this country, the rapid changes in the weather and the light, and Patsy knew how much it pleased most of the visitors. She concentrated on thinking of some safe but appealing routes on which to take them.

Katy was out in the yard when she got back, perched on the large piece of rock which acted as a mounting block. She was drinking coffee and listening to her radio and as Patsy stopped Golly beside her she heard the regular hoofbeats of a trotting horse coming from the field. She turned Golly to investigate and saw the bay pony trotting a rhythmic circle and moving on to a steady canter while behind her the beat of Katy's music seemed almost to fit.

For a moment Patsy could not believe what she was seeing but then the music stopped as Katy turned off the radio and the pony came back to a trot, saw Golly, and turned to the gate to meet him.

'Katy, that pony, he was working with the music,' Patsy told her and Katy came to stare.

'Put your radio back on,' Patsy told her and Katy did so but the music had changed to something with no strong beat and the pony took no notice, merely reaching over the gate to sniff at Golly.

'Sure you didn't imagine it?' asked Katy, and Patsy said that she must have done. The bay certainly did not look a likely circus pony in spite of the white lock of mane.

CHAPTER THREE.

There was a mare coming tomorrow to be covered by Hedfa Aur. She would be turned out first next to him to give the stallion time to get used to her and to wait for her to be ready, then she and Goliath would change places. There were risks to this method, the mare might kick or she might kick the stallion but it was a more natural way than to have Hedfa Aur serve her in hand and they both had their shoes off to make a kick less damaging.

They had used the method twice before the previous year when the stallion was only just mature enough and all had been well. Patsy hoped that it would be again, although it was a shame that Gareth was away for a few days but Katy would be at home.

The visitor was a section C mare, another chestnut, the smaller type known as a pony of cob type. She arrived in a trailer towed by a Land Rover and Hedfa Aur arrived at the gate to watch in his usual imperious way. He always considered anything that happened to be his business. He greeted the new arrival with his challenging shriek and the little mare responded with an answering whinny, her tail immediately promisingly raised. Her owner, a middle-aged lady who bred a few foals each year as a hobby, laughed.

'I think madame is going to like him,' she said. 'She can be fussy, tells the boys to clear off if she doesn't take to them, and we had no luck having her covered in hand. These ponies are best when things are natural.'

Gareth had put up an electric fence to give the mare a run between the stallion's field and the one occupied by Eithin Aur and Osbourne and the mare's owner put her straight out there. The stallion pranced up, very interested, and after a flirtatious squeal the pony turned her back to investigate the grass and the two horses on her other side who had come to watch.

'We'll give them time to settle and if it looks promising I'll let her through,' Patsy told the owner.

She offered coffee but the lady said that she needed to get back and Patsy watched her drive out.

'There you are,' she told the empty air. 'Just how you wanted it.'

There was no stir of air, no feeling that there was anything in the yard apart from herself and two of the cats sunning themselves on the rock they used for mounting, and Patsy knew that she was alone. Whatever it was with which she had once felt a connection was no longer there.

By next morning things looked promising. The mare had been in for the night in case of trouble and she was now close to the tape, her tail flirtatiously up, turned towards the stallion who was impatiently pawing the ground. It was obviously only the threat of a shock: that was keeping them safely away from the main fence and Patsy phoned Katy who came to help.

Goliath, looking resigned, was brought in and Katy held the stallion back while Patsy let the mare into his field. There was some squealing and flirting but although young Hedfa Aur took charge, the pony accepted his determined advances, and Patsy knew that her stud fee, if all went well, would be earned. The mare would stay with him for a few days until it seemed sure that she was bred and then long-suffering Goliath would go back as the stallion's security.

All went as planned and the pony was collected by her owner. Hedfa Aur seemed to accept her going without being too disturbed although he did warn Golly to keep his distance when he took her place. The bay pony watched these coming and goings with mild interest. He did not show any signs of needing a field companion himself but Patsy planned to change that.

'When Mack gets back we'll need a companion for Goldie,' she told Katy. 'Best to leave the trekkers separate. If that pony's still here we'll try him out with her.'

'I don't suppose he's going anywhere,' Katy went to speak to him and he pushed his nose into her shoulder in his usual way and Patsy knew that it was a sensible idea. She might be glad when Mack got home again but Osbourne had been useful.

'Let's see how civilised he is,' said Katy 'I'll get the lunge rein and we'll give him a test.'

The pony did not seem to mind the lunging cavesson being put on his head. They had made a small schooling ring behind the stables, surfaced by a load of sand from the local quarry, and Katy led him into it and clipped on the long webbing line. She bent to pick up the lunging whip and as she straightened up with it the pony's ears went back, his head went up, and he shot forward, tucking in his tail.

'Drop it,' Patsy shouted. 'Drop the whip Katy.'

The pony was swinging out wildly at the end of the rein, almost pulling it out of Katy's hand, and Katy did as her mother said and dropped the long-lashed whip, there to be used to instruct the pony to keep out and go forward to gentle signals. For a moment the pony kept going but Katy told him 'walk...walking...steady...' and he began to respond. After a couple of scared circuits he slowed, dropped to a walk, and swung round to stare at Katy.

'Call him in,' said Patsy quietly, and Katy did so. After a moment of staring and snorting the pony relaxed, lowered his head, and walked quietly to her, and Katy rubbed his head and talked to him.

'He's whip shy,' she said, and Patsy agreed.

'Try him without the whip,' she suggested, and Katy turned the pony back onto the circle and let out the rein, telling him to walk on, and he obeyed, nervously at first, but gradually relaxing. Soon he was trotting obediently on either rein and he still behaved in canter. Katy called him in and patted him.

'We'd better give him a bit longer and then I'll try riding him,' she said, and Patsy agreed.

'But we'll have to be careful,' she said. 'He could be dangerous.'

'He certainly doesn't look it,' Katy fondled the pony.

'He's a sweetie. He was just afraid that I was going to beat him.'

It was time to try the new ponies. They came in easily and she and Katy saddled them. Again it was the grey pony who was less stolid, flattening her ears when her girth was tightened and putting her head in the air when Katy bridled her. Katy grinned.

'I'll ride this one,' she stated. 'You can have the easy one.'

'I hope they'll both be easy when we get out,' said Patsy. 'Otherwise they won't be much good for trekkers.'

The two ponies stood quietly to be mounted and Katy led the way out past the cattle grid. The grey pony seemed to expect to be in the lead, she walked out briskly, ears pricked, and Patsy's ride tucked in behind. On the short stretch of road before the moor they met a milk tanker which slowed down to pass them and neither pony seemed to mind.

They had obviously seen open moorland before. With the grey still determinedly in the lead they did a short loop down a worn track to a narrow wooden bridge with one single rail. The stream below was running high after the winter rains, cascading between some rocks, but after a glance down the ponies accepted the crossing. They trotted and cantered round the green beyond, watched by scattered sheep and two of the mountain ponies and turned back onto the track. Katy patted Cinders, her grey, and Patsy pushed Sweep up to go alongside.

'They seem fine,' Katy said. 'This one's quite willing,

yours looks a bit stuffy.'

He's a follower,' Patsy rubbed her pony's neck under his thick mane. 'But that's just what we need for trekkers.'

'They won't be complete beginners will they?' asked Katy, and Patsy said no.

'They must be able to steer a bit and rise to the trot,' she said. 'We'll give them ten minutes in the school first to check it out and if they don't look safe I'll have to say so.'

It was a beautiful day, warm for early May. The swallows were chattering on the phone line and swooping in and out of the buildings and after putting the ponies back in their field Patsy felt restless.

'Have you got to work this afternoon?' she asked Katy, who shook her head.

'Nothing that won't wait,' she told her mother. 'And Gareth isn't here. Why?'

'Let's take them to the beach,' suggested Patsy. 'They both love it and it won't be crowded this early in the season. If we don't go before the visitors arrive we won't get many chances.'

Katy agreed enthusiastically and they collected Golly and the mare. Patsy backed the Transit out of its' parking spot while Katy saddled the horses and they loaded up and set off. This was another of the things that Mack would be missing, she thought, he and Osbourne loved the beach, and she was glad that she had Katy to share it with.

The journey took about twenty minutes. The nearest beach was at Newport and the road down to it sloped steeply downhill across a cattle grid and a golf course. The bay was spread out in front of them as they drove down, a stretch of sparkling water with the cliffs dropping down at the nearer end and at the other the sand dunes and the wide beach led to the point where the marshes of the estuary spread out as the river entered the sea.

Parking was right by the beach and there was a ramp down to the sand. Both horses knew where they were, they came out of the lorry eagerly, and Patsy held the mare's head while Katy got on board before she mounted the more patient Goliath. Golly had been astonished by his first trip to the beach; Patsy remembered his doubts about the soft sand under his feet and his snorting horror at the sight of the white breaking foam, but she had first taken him there in company with Osbourne and his completely imperturbable rider. Now he understood that the whole, open, gleaming expanse, the moving, flashing water, and the wheeling gulls meant fun and he followed Goldie happily to the water's edge.

They trotted first, heading along the edge of the surf towards the creek and the small town beyond. The mare went with her exaggerated cob trot, sending the sandy water flying, and Golly kept beside her, pulling for freedom to go faster. As the beach turned inwards to the dunes Katy turned Goldie the other way, down the spit of sand between creek and sea until they were surrounded on three sides by the water, and for a minute they stopped, both horses gazing out to sea, and then Katy looked at her mother and grinned.

'Here goes,' she said, and swung Eithin Aur back to face towards the open sand and the cliffs at the other end.

Patsy felt Golly's hocks come under him as he turned and then they were away in the flying spray at the water's edge. The two horses were well matched, they galloped together, and the water flew up into the rider's faces, cold and salt and invigorating. The wind was still cold and the few people on the beach, mostly dog walkers, stood back to watch. An excited terrier gave chase for a few strides but neither horse took any notice and the dog soon fell back.

There was a low brake water ahead and Katy swung a few yards inwards to face it and her powerful little cob hopped neatly over. Patsy turned Golly for it and felt his eager snatch at the bit. Goliath had been a great show jumper in Katy's pony club days and he still loved to jump. He took off in one of his bold leaps and put on a spurt on landing in an attempt to catch up with his friend and for a few strides Patsy completely let him go, but the beach ahead was turning rocky as they neared the cliffs and Katy was starting to pull up. As Golly came alongside both horses dropped back to an unwilling trot and Patsy found that she was laughing. She had enjoyed many things about living alone at Bryn Uchaf but she had to admit that at times she had been lonely. Since Katy and Gareth had found her ill and rescued her that had changed, although she had tried hard not to impose on Katy and Gareth too much. Katy had lived with her for a time, until she and Gareth had decided that things were serious between them, and the idea of converting the old stables into a cottage had seemed a good solution.

'After all, if we don't last you could use it for holiday lets,' Katy had said, and Patsy had agreed.

Now they turned the horses back to the sea and let them splash and paw, sending fountain of water over their chests and their rider's legs, before they went back to the lorry. The horses were relaxed now, even the usually impatient Goldie happy to stand to be unsaddled and then to follow Golly back up the ramp.

'I enjoyed that,' said Katy happily as Patsy drove slowly back up the narrow road across the golf course. 'When I first knew her Goldie was still half wild but look at her today, positively civilised.'

'She's settled,' replied Patsy. 'A bit like you, sensible home-based job and married.'

'Yes,' Katy sounded suddenly surprised. 'I suppose that is me now, settled and sensible. Whoever would have thought it.'

"I wouldn't have" thought Patsy, but she did not say so. It had certainly seemed to be what Katy had come to want, and she was glad for her. She just hoped that it would last.

Both horses needed hosing down after their trip to the beach. Golly loved to be washed, he leaned into the stream of water and half closed his eyes while Patsy washed and brushed the sticky salt and sand from his legs and stomach. The mare was not so keen and Katy held onto her while Patsy did the washing.

'It won't be good enough to satisfy them,' said Katy.

'Just watch them roll.'
She was right. Back in their fields both of them went straight down, Goldie after carefully digging her spot, Golly with a thankful sigh. Hedfa Aur and Osbourne watched the waving legs, Osbourne indulgently and the stallion poised ready to go down and mark his territory by rolling in the same spot as soon as Golly got up. The bay pony watched and when he was up the stallion trotted across to lean over the fence and nuzzle and squeal at him. The pony refused to be involved, he turned away and walked back to his most usual standing place by the gate and Patsy knew with sad certainty that it was a person that he was waiting for.

It was still early enough in the year for it to go cold on a clear evening. After the horses were fed
Patsy went in to get her tea and join the old cat by the Rayburn. Her grown up kittens were out hunting but the mother had spent too many cold nights with no cosy shelter in the days when her master had gone and the house had spent months empty before Patsy came. Emrys's house had not sold easily, its history had left a shadow which Patsy had only discovered after she bought it, in a reckless gamble on finding the home and life that had always been her secret dream.

It was some time later, when she was on her way to bed, that Patsy heard galloping. The horses did sometimes run at night but usually in short, playful bursts but this was different. Patsy pulled her sweater back on and went to investigate.

It was a cold, still, shining night, a full moon sending

deep shadows and a strange light like filtered sunlight over the fields and the half-fledged trees beyond. For a moment, as Patsy made her way across the yard to the field, nothing moved except one of the cats slipping out of the shadows to join her, and then the galloping started again. It was the bay pony, circling his field, a swiftly moving silhouette with the white patch on his neck looking almost like a hand on a rein. He came past Patsy fast, his tail catching sparks of moonlight, and Patsy heard his fast breathing and smelled the trampled grass. It was unreal, and for a moment she almost thought that she was dreaming, and then Katy's voice behind her said 'what on earth is up with him?' and her daughter was beside her, a coat thrown over her nightdress.

'I don't know,' Patsy was glad to find everything dropping back to normal. It was no longer a moment out of time, something elemental in the moonlight and this ancient, magic land, it was just a spooked horse, possibly with colic, to be checked and soothed.

The other horses were taking no notice, grazing calmly in the moonlight, and Patsy said, 'We need to try to catch him and have a look.'

'I'll get some nuts, see if he'll come for them,' said Katy.

The pony seemed to register that they were there. He came back to a trot and as Katy came back and shook the bucket he stopped and stood for a moment staring at them. He was breathing hard but he did not look distressed and now he shook his head and walked across to them at the gate. He pushed his head under Katy's arm, rubbing, and then his attention turned to the food and he plunged his nose into the bucket. Patsy ran a hand under his mane; he was sweating, the warmth steaming from him now in the cold air, but he ate happily and then stayed quietly beside them as Katy patted him.

'I don't think there's anything wrong,' she said. 'Perhaps he was excited by the moonlight.'

The pony shook his head and snorted and then moved away, nosing at the grass, and Katy pulled her coat round her and shivered. 'It's freezing out here,' she said. 'I'm going back to bed. Gareth will have something to say about my cold feet.'

She turned away but Patsy stayed for a minute, watching the pony. He seemed quite calm now, nibbling the short, sweet new grass as a wisp of cloud drifted across the moon, making it suddenly very dark. Patsy shivered herself and turned towards the lights of her house. It had been a strange moment but strange things were part of living in this land, where ancient cromlechs marked the landscape and once the bluestones had been quarried and mysteriously transported hundreds of miles to Stonehenge.

CHAPTER FOUR.

Safe in her own hidden world Sylva dreamed that she was riding, bareback on her galloping pony. There was a strange, shimmering half light and a feeling of space and freedom. The pony's neck was warm under her hands, his mane lifting in the breeze of his gallop, there was no one else, no one to mock or make her angry, nothing mattered except this wonderful feeling of one-ness with the creature that she loved.

CHAPTER FIVE.

Two days later Rhianne rang to say that she had two ladies who would like to ride.
'They both ride regularly at a riding school,' she said, and Patsy agreed to take them out. Katy was working and she decided that she would take them out by herself. Golly was already in as she had been planning to ride him later and it did not take long to catch Cinders and Sweep and brush them over.
The ladies arrived while she was still saddling up and offered to help. They said that they were friends holidaying together and that their husbands were playing golf at the Newport golf club which Patsy knew was well known and very scenic.
Watching them ride round the ring Patsy was glad to see that they were both competent riders. Sweep still followed his friend and the lady on him laughed.
'I don't think I'll be getting lost anyway,' she said and Patsy knew that her first trekkers understood horses. Feeling relieved she mounted Golly and led the way out.
The ride was a success. Patsy took what she thought of as a medium ride, involving some climbing and ditches to get through or over and a safe green stretch

for a canter. Golly accepted the new order, going steadily in the lead and laying back his ears In warning to Cinders when she considered coming past him. The ladies exclaimed about the scenery and were delighted when the route took them past a group of wild ponies with several very new foals. They got home with no dramas and the ladies said they would like to ride again before their holiday ended. Patsy turned the ponies out feeling satisfied. She had enjoyed the new venture; it was a change and she had enjoyed the enthusiasm of the ladies and the chance to show them these little known hills.

Katy was quite jealous when she heard that she had missed their first trek and was stirred to decide to try something new herself.

'I'm going to ride the pony,' she said that afternoon.' Goldie's tack should fit him.'

'The saddle will be too wide,' guessed Patsy. 'It's a cob width, the pony is quite narrow.'

'David's then,' Katy took the cover off the neat looking little saddle and paused for a moment holding it.

'I had some fun on him in this,' she said nostalgically. 'He was such a willing little horse.'

Patsy agreed. Little David had been fun, quick and clever and up for anything. It was always sad that horses had such comparatively short lives, but this pony was still alive. She wondered if someone, perhaps the person he seemed to be watching for, was missing him as well or had something happened to them?

The saddle was a bit small but it did not look likely

to pinch. Katy took stirrups and girths off the mare's saddle and her martingale off the bridle and Patsy followed her to the pony's stable.

He was good to tack up, accepting the snaffle bit in his mouth and not showing any resentment when Katy pulled up the girth. She led him out and he stood at the mounting block until she was settled in the saddle and Patsy opened the gate to let them into the schooling ring.

The pony was nervous, going in fits and starts at first and turning his ears back anxiously to check his rider. Katy sat quietly, her reins loose and a hand gentling his neck, and gradually he relaxed.

'He's had a rough time somewhere,' she told Patsy, stopping beside her where she was leaning on the gate.

'But not from whoever it is he's watching for,' said Patsy. The pony turned his head to sniff his rider's foot, and Katy leaned forward and let him sniff her hand as well. The pony seemed reassured, he settled to walk and trot round more steadily and Katy pulled up again, patting him

'He's nice,' she said. 'He's obviously been roughly treated at some time but he seems to settle. Next time let's try taking him out with Golly.'

Patsy agreed. 'He needs a name, if he's going to be staying,' she said. 'He can't go on being 'the pony.'

'How about Castaway?' suggested Katy. 'It's what he was. Cass for short.'

She got off and the pony rubbed his head on her and Patsy nodded.

'I like it,' she said, and knew that for now, anyway, the pony was an official resident.

CHAPTER SIX.

Miles away, in the small white room and the small white hospital bed, the screen on the bedside monitor showed a green graph, a steady rhythm ticking away on it. The fair-haired young man at the bedside looked at it and sighed. They had told him that his sister was stable, still deep in the coma as she had been now for weeks. He could not stay any longer, he squeezed the unresponsive hand, paused, and looked down at the still, white face and the pale, straw coloured hair so like his own. She had always been quiet, close to him but always keeping something back, something that only relaxed when she was with her beloved pony.

It seemed that they would never know quite what had happened to her on the day she had been found lying at the roadside and her horse had come home alone and traumatised with blood on his legs. There had been skid marks on the road which looked as if he had bolted but he had never done such a thing before, he had learned to trust Sylva so completely that they almost seemed to share their thoughts.

'I must go now Syl,' he told her softly. 'I'll be back, just hang on there, please don't drift any further away.'

SOLE POSSESSION

She was his twin, without her he only felt half there. He turned to the door as it opened and a nurse came in.

'Is there any change?' he asked, knowing what the answer would be, and the nurse smiled sympathetically. All the staff knew about the Lynton twins and were sorry for this anxious young man, at seventeen little more than a boy. He was Sylva Lynton's only regular visitor these days, their mother having found her daughter's state impossible to cope with.

'She dreamed again the other night,' the nurse told him. 'That's always a hopeful sign, but then she sank back. Is there anything you know of that she might dream about? Whatever it is doesn't seem to upset her.'

'Horses,' he replied. 'Her pony, she'd always loved horses, especially the one she was riding when this happened. I've tried talking about them to her, but she doesn't respond.'

'Keep trying,' the nurse said. 'You never know.'

In her closed off private world Sylva stood beside her pony, stroking his neck, the clear, blue air around them as he leaned into her. There was nothing else, no past or future, just this cocoon of peace and one-ness with this animal whom she could reach and understand as she never had been able to do with a human. Something horrible had happened, she did not want to remember what, for now she would just dream with her pony.

The nurse moved on to the bedside and Simon went out. He had homework to do with exams coming up, he would go home to the house on the exclusive estate and work in his room. His mother was away as she frequently was, filming the soap in which she had a long-term starring role, and the housekeeping couple who lived in would not bother him. He might even have time later for making some music. It seemed ages since he had last had time for his keyboard.

CHAPTER SEVEN.

The first of Hedfa Aur's visiting mares went home safely in foal and another was due to arrive. The stallion knew what is was about when she was led out of the lorry and by the time her owner drove off he was pacing about near the gate.

'He's going to get harder to handle,' said Gareth, watching the stallion pace alongside the fence with arched neck and tense loins when they had put the mare out in her strip next door. 'Da says you or Katy could get hurt, and Katy...' he stopped, a quick smile on his face, and Patsy wondered if her daughter had some news about which she was keeping quiet. She would hear soon enough if she was right.

'I don't think we need to wait before putting the mare in,' she said now, and Gareth agreed.

'I'll get your cob,' he said. 'While the boy's busy chatting up the mare, no need for you to get in with them.' He caught Golly, who was looking resigned, and then got hold of the stallion while Patsy let the mare through. Hedfa Aur was not prepared to wait, he almost knocked Gareth over before setting off to round up the coquettish mare, and Patsy knew that there was some sense in the idea of sending the stallion away to work at a professional cob stud, but ridiculously she also knew that it would seem like letting Emrys down.

The weather seemed to have settled, the evenings were long and luminous, and that evening, having seen Katy and Gareth drive off to meet some friends for a drink, Patsy decided to take Golly for a ride on the mountain. The sun was low, sinking west towards the sea, and the sky was striped in a drift of light grey and gold which she knew would lead to a brilliant sunset. There would just be time to watch it from halfway up the Hafod, the summer sheep grazing, and get back again before it grew too dark to reach the gate at the end of her lane.

Golly went up the track in the growing golden glow which was like fire on the grass and on the gorse bushes. Reaching the single Rowan tree which marked the halfway point Patsy pulled him up and turned to watch.

The sky was on fire, crimson and gold edged with green, the light too bright to see anything but shadows at ground level. Golly stood with pricked ears, seeming to watch as well, while the colours and the light began to fade as the last rim of the sun dropped into the flaming sea. It was time to get home. Patsy was almost level with the gates off the moor when movement at the further gate caught her eye. There was a dark shadow outside the gate, a vehicle of some sort, and shadows moved onto the moor. A pony whinnied and she saw a group of them becoming moving shadows, and she also saw one separate shape moving towards them as the gate rattled shut. Suddenly Patsy guessed what she was seeing...another pony being dumped. Turning the reluctant Golly away from the path to home she sent him into a canter along the side of the moor but she heard a vehicle start up and as it moved away she had only an impression of a smallish lorry with a flash of something white on its dark paint before it was out of sight.

The grey stallion was already on his way to inspect the newcomer and from his approach Patsy guessed that it was a mare. In the thickening dusk she could see that it was small and hairy, possibly a Shetland, and she knew that she would have to leave them to it. If it was taken into the herd it would probably be alright; the weather was warmer and the farmers would spot it in a few days and decide what to do. She would tell Gareth's father, he would spread the word. For now it was time to get Golly home before the short stretch of road become quite dark.

'But who would keep dumping ponies like this?' wondered Katy when Patsy told her. 'If they've got several why not put them out in one go, less risk of being caught.'

Patsy had wondered that as well and come up with no possible answers, but Gareth said, 'somewhere there must be money in it, either saved or paid,' but none of them could think how.

The dumped pony was a Shetland, Patsy saw it again a few days later when she and Katy were out for a short ride with Katy on Cass. It was chestnut, thin and unkempt, but it seemed to have been accepted by the herd although it was a few yards away from the main group.

'It'll probably be alright,' said Katy. 'It'll come in later in the year, when the owners check the ponies, and what would happen to it anyway if we did catch it? We can't adopt them all.'

Patsy knew that she was right, there were too many unwanted ponies and this one could be as well off out here as anywhere. Shetlands were tough, a quite different proposition to Cass.

The bay pony seemed to have accepted that Katy was not going to hurt him. He was mainly unfazed by the moor. He was hesitant about the plank bridge with the single rail which was the way across the most undercut stream but he followed Golly across, snorting at the fast moving water flowing under it. It was a warm day and he sweated, obviously unfit, and he was willing if sometimes jumpy, but he seemed to have no idea of being deliberately difficult.

'I don't get it,' said Katy, when they got home. 'Why would anyone dump him? Surely he'd sell.'

'Perhaps he's unsound,' Patsy leaned on the gate to watch as the pony moved away, and Katy said 'he certainly didn't feel it, but it could be something subtle. We'll find out if it is. I expect he's here to stay anyway.'

Checking for a microchip had shown nothing.

'All Horses are supposed to be chipped but a lot still aren't,' the vet told Patsy. He had visited to do the annual flu jabs for Golly and Osbourne and he gave Mack's big old horse a parting pat.

'Mack still away at sea?' he asked and Patsy said that he was. The vet laughed.

'Bet he isn't too happy,' he said. 'Sitting on one of those skyscrapers on water won't be much to his taste but Tabitha likes a bit of the good life.'

He went back to his car and Patsy, preparing to lead Osbourne back to his field, knew that he was right.

In the next field Hedfa Aur looked peaceful with his latest mare. The two mares he had covered last season were due to foal and Patsy was hoping for good news of them. Soon the season for covering would be over and Katy would start to ride him again and get ready for the agricultural shows and for the Royal Welsh, the summit of the Welsh farming and equestrian year. They had enjoyed them last year, with the stallion, still in the youngster classes, beginning to show his worth culminating in his huge success at the Royal Welsh.

'He's looking good,' Katy too was leaning on the fence looking at the bright golden little horse. 'How many more mares has he got booked?'

'That's the lot for this year,' Patsy told her. 'That's enough for us to cope with. It'll be hay time soon, I want to keep the big back field closed off until it's cut and we'll be getting short of grazing if we have too many visitors.'

'That's when standing him away would help,' said Katy but Patsy did not intend to change her mind.

'We need to get his show entries in,' she said, and Katy nodded.

'I want to try him under saddle,' she said. 'Watching

Gareth run might be quite a turn on but I don't like always being on the sidelines. I really fancy riding him at the Royal Welsh this year.'

'We could give it a try,' Patsy liked the idea. 'There's the local young farmers show coming up, how about giving it a go in that?'

'Yes,' Katy was enthusiastic. 'I'd like to get some more competitive miles, its ages since I used to jump Golly. Talking of which, let's give the old boy a jump now. I reckon Fly would jump, especially if he was gelded.'

'I couldn't do that to him,' Patsy imagined her majestic little horse with his pride tamed. There might be problems with handling so much testosterone but she could never do that to him.

Katy, suddenly enthusiastic, was hauling their few crates and poles out into the middle of the school to make three simple jumps and Patsy saddled Golly for her. It was a long time since the elderly cob's glory days, winning jumping and hunter trial classes so regularly that other competitors sighed when they saw him coming, but he had not forgotten. With Katy on his back, business like and eager with her stirrups shortened, he was immediately rejuvenated, keen and gathered with pricked ears, and Patsy watched with a feeling of nostalgia as her daughter, looking about sixteen again on the eager cob, let him bound forward to the first jump.

Golly had not forgotten what to do, he had always loved it and it was clear that he still did. Katy went over the poles several times and pulled up laughing.

'That felt good,' she said.

She was still jumping a few minutes later when Gareth, who had been dealing with a problem for one of his I.T. clients, drove in and came to the gate to watch. Patsy had put the last rails up as high as her makeshift stands would allow and Golly was heading for them all eager bounce. He did his trademark explosive spring and Katy, out of practise, was briefly unseated. Patsy heard Gareth catch his breath and when Katy, still laughing, stopped by the gate he said, 'Katy...'
'What?' she demanded. 'I've been re-living old times. I'll be there in five minutes, as you're obviously in a rush.'
She jumped off the puffing horse and Patsy, sensing trouble, took him from her.
'He was a good boy,' she said. 'I'll see to him, you go in.' Gareth had turned away, heading for their cottage, and Katy gave Golly a final pat and followed him. Patsy heard the door slam and the sound of raised voices and let Golly rub his sweaty head on her shoulder. Whatever the problem was she was wise enough to keep out of it.
After lunch, when Katy had gone home to do some work, Patsy went for one of her regular walks down through the early summer woods and over her stream to follow its bank along to the place where the grass and bushes opened out and the outcrop of towering rocks sheltered a small, empty partly collapsed cottage. A white egret rose silently from a quiet pool beside the water where Patsy knew that trout often lay. It rose a little uncertainly into the air and Patsy saw that it had a damaged wing. It was unusual to see

egrets here, at this sheltered stream, although they nested on the Newport reed beds closer to the sea. She wondered if it been chased by other birds because of the damaged wing. This spot was a quiet sanctuary and the water here was close to the healing stones which were the exact match to the smaller stones of Stonehenge. There had to have been some reason for early man to have transported those stones on that incredibly difficult journey and it was likely that the legendary healing power was a reason. It had only recently been discovered that this was the exact spot from which some of those stones had come. For a time there had been visits from groups of archaeologists but active interest had faded and now Patsy had this silent spot to herself. The silvery grey cliff rose behind her as she sat on one of the fallen rocks facing the swiftly flowing stream and the bank of her own freshly leafed trees beyond it. There was the great sense of stillness and time common to all the ancient spots and Patsy imagined that she could feel the presence of an energy as old as the planet.

Something moved on the bank of the stream and for a moment Patsy saw the quick, sinuous shape of an otter. It glided a bit closer, caught her scent, and vanished as quickly as it had appeared. Conscious that her human presence was disturbing the spot Patsy stood up to walk back and saw the otter slide back into the water but the feel of that place was something which always remained quietly with her.

Cass seemed to have settled. He put on some condition and Katy rode him a few times in the field when she was not using her riding time to school Goldie. The mare would always be quick and headstrong, she had been almost unhandled when Patsy had bought her, in foal to Emrys's great Highflyer, as a four year old from Llanybydder horse sales. She could quickly panic and try to take off and Katy could never relax while riding her, but she enjoyed the challenge although she said that riding Cass was quite a rest cure.

The first trekkers had gone but it was not long before some more holiday makers wanted to ride.

This time it was less straight forward. There were two adults and two children. The adults had ridden very little but the children had regular lessons and the ten year old boy said that he wanted to gallop.

'We'll have to offer two rides,' Patsy told Rhianne. 'A shortish one starting in the school for the adults then something a bit more for the children.'

This worked quite well. The adults had ridden very little and were quite happy with a few minutes in the school followed by the adventure of a short trip on the moor with Katy on foot walking with them.

When they returned Patsy, hoping to avoid trouble, put the boy on Sweep and his older sister on Cinders and mounted Golly herself. As she had hoped Sweep had no intention of passing his friend, he ignored flapping legs and reins and Patsy was firm with his rider about using rough aids.

'If this is really going to be popular we could do with another pony,' said Katy. 'I'll have to ride Cass more and see if he'll settle.

Hedfa Aur's last mare went home and the hay began to

grow high and flower. The weather was unsettled, warm days giving way to brief spells of soaking rain, and Patsy hoped that it would settle in time to get the hay safely cut.

One sultry June morning when the flies were too bad for schooling to be comfortable Katy proposed to try a ride out on Cass round the quiet lanes and bridleways which lay on the opposite side to the moor. The flies were still annoying but both horses were well sprayed with repellent and glad to be in the shade.

The primroses were long over, and the bluebells, and the tall spikes of foxgloves were taking their place in the long grass under the green hedges. The horses swished their tails and tossed their heads at the flies and Katy said that it would rain again soon.

'It always starts raining when the shows get nearer,' she said. 'The most lively bit of the year, but it has to spoil them.'

She sounded restless and Patsy risked a careful probe.

'Are you going to be here for all of them?' she asked. 'What about a holiday?'

'Gareth wants to go to Spain,' Katy told her. 'I said we'd need to be here for the hay and I didn't want to miss the big shows but he says I need to take it easy for a bit.'

'You hardly ever relax', Patsy told her. 'You're always revving yourself up about something.'

'That's what he says,' Katy sounded resentful. 'He reckons that's why...'

She stopped but Patsy carried on. 'Why you don't start that baby,' she said and Katy rounded on her.

'You're just as bad,' she said. 'You and his wretched mother. You'd think I was a sheep, or a brood mare. Anyway...' she stopped suddenly.

'It was the reason you decided to actually get married,' Patsy reminded her, and Katy said 'Maybe I got carried away, it all seemed so idyllic, sweet couple making a family for everyone to admire. I should have known it wasn't that easy.'

'You don't really regret marrying Gareth do you?' Patsy hoped she was no going too far but before Katy had time to snap at her they met the dogs.

They had turned for home down the edge of the green behind the group of cottages which formed the local village and the dogs came from behind them. There were two of them, two quite big black and white dogs with a look of pointers, and they were obviously on the loose and looking for trouble. The horses tensed, startled, as a man, obviously the dogs' owner, came round the corner shouting, a lead and a stick in his hands.

The dogs came straight at the horses, ignoring their owner's threatening stick, and Katy started to turn Cass to face them and raised her own stick threateningly. Cass was immediately terrified. He spun back in the direction in which they had been heading, his ears went back and his tail in, and he dived forward.

'Hang on,' Patsy had shortened her reins and was preparing to turn Golly in an attempt to drive the dogs off, but Cass did not hesitate. He was off down the sloping track as the dogs, finding their owner close and threatening, gave up their chase and turned back, heads down and suddenly submissive as he grabbed their collars.

'Sorry,' he called. 'Someone left my gate open, I'm so sorry.'

Patsy did not wait. Golly, disturbed and excited, was bouncing sideways trying to follow Cass, and from the clatter ahead she knew that Cass had reached the road.

Golly went down the rough track at a scrambling canter and Patsy heard a screech of tyres and a blast on a horn as someone obviously met the runaway.

Afraid of what she might find Patsy turned off the common into the road and saw her daughter and the pony further down, Katy on her feet, hanging onto the terrified pony and trying to calm him. Golly shouted a relieved greeting and Cass turned to stare at him as he and Patsy slid to a stop nearby. The pony was lathered white and shaking and Katy looked much the same.

'Are you alright?' Patsy asked her and Katy said shakily that she was.

'I managed to turn him into the hedge,' she said. 'Was it the dogs, or the sticks he was so scared of? He wasn't panicking at first, it was when I raised my stick he went off on one.'

'I don't know,' Patsy was just relieved to see them both in one piece. 'We do know he's scared of whips.'

'He was certainly right off his head,' Katy was gentling the pony, rubbing his neck as he turned his head towards her. 'There was a car, I thought we were going right into it.'

Her voice was still unsteady and Patsy said, 'Best lead him home, just in case. It seems we've found the reason he was dumped.'

'I ought to get on again,' Katy sounded unconvinced and Patsy got off Golly.

'I'll walk with him,' she said 'Sitting on Golly will be good for your nerve, and we don't know what that one would do if we met another dog.'

Katy agreed and Patsy took Cass's rein from her. It was only a short walk back to Bryn Uchaf but by the time they reached it Patsy was glad to be home.

Katy seemed to have recovered, it was not her first near miss with horses, and Cass too seemed to have got over his fright.

'Gareth can bring Shep and Dai over, see if he minds them,' suggested Katy. 'He might be scared anyway if he connects dogs with that fright,' and Patsy agreed that it was a good idea.

'We're going to need to be careful about riding him,' she said. 'If it was the stick then the answer's easy, don't carry one, but we mustn't start trusting him. That bolt could have been lethal.'

Out in the field again Cass seemed back to normal. He had a luxurious roll in some mud and moved away to graze. Katy stretched her arms and said that they ached.

'He's pretty strong,' she told Patsy. 'I'll be stiff tomorrow, I'm going to go in and have a bath.'

She went off and in the field the pony raised his head for a moment and looked round.

'It's alright, no dogs or sticks,' Patsy assured him, but

Cass was watching Katy until she was out of sight before he went back to grazing. Patsy decided that her daughter had the right idea and she headed in for hot water and some scented bath essence herself.

CHAPTER EIGHT.

In the hospital room Simón looked sadly down at his sister. She looked no different, still and shut away from him in some distant place of her own. Beside him the nurse said, 'She got very agitated, rolling her head from side to side and trying to say something. Her eyelids were fluttering, we wondered if she was going to wake up...or something else. Doctor said we should call you.'

'But now she doesn't seem any different,' said Simon, and the nurse agreed.

'But even dreaming is a good sign,' she said. 'Do you want to stay with her for a bit? You never know, something happened.'

'I'll stay,' Simon told her. When the nurse had gone, leaving the line on the screen still steady, he sat down and took his sister's unresponsive hand.

'What is it Syl?' he asked her. 'Where are you, why can't I reach you? We used to be so close before...'

He stopped, switching off the memory of that quarrel, the only real quarrel he and his twin had ever had, when she had accused him of invading her mind because he was jealous of that man she was becoming obsessed with, that creepy Drake, with his flashy riding and his hand always touching her.

Drake had been the yard's Idol with his two show jumpers and his sleek looks but after Silva's accident he had suddenly moved his horses to livery somewhere else and gone. Simon had wondered if there was any connection but he had no idea what it could be.

He had tried to reach her in their old childhood way, but she had blocked him out, seeming only close to her pony, and before he could try to put things right this had happened.

'I'm sorry,' he told her now, not for the first time, but he knew that she could not hear him. Sighing, he settled to watch over her.

CHAPTER NINE.

Cass seemed to have settled again. Gareth, muttering about the dangers of riding, which never seemed to have worried him before, brought the farm collies over and let him snort and sniff at them but he did not seem worried. Watching him as he reached for a mouthful of grass with them close by Patsy said 'he isn't bothered. I think it was your stick and the one the man had that scared him.'
'He'll be fine now,' Katy told them. 'But I'll give him a bit of time. I've got plenty to do getting Fly back into riding mood.'
'And I suppose a working stallion is more reliable,' stated Gareth, calling his exploring dogs back to heel as the cats looked on resentfully from safe perches. 'You did agree to being careful Katy.'
'And I am,' Katy sounded defensive. 'I won't ride Cass again if it bothers you so much.'
Patsy suddenly knew that her suspicion was right and as Gareth headed back across the field with his dogs she looked at Katy.
'I take it you've got some news?' she asked and Katy stared at her, looking suddenly scared.
'Yes,' she said. 'I am, I'm pregnant and...and I'm scared

stiff and he won't let me forget about it. Oh Mum, what's it like? Will I have to spend months feeling sick and weird, and will it hurt? I never really thought about it before, but I was sick this morning, it was horrible.'

'That'll stop,' Patsy told her hopefully. 'And having it is a tremendous experience, you'll have plenty of help, we aren't in Victorian times. You've no need to be scared.'

'Gareth's so thrilled,' Katy told her. 'He wants to tell Rhianne and John, but I don't want everyone fussing. I shall feel like a prize cow or something.'

'You can hardly keep hiding it,' Patsy pointed out. 'And I think it's wonderful news. After all, it's why you decided to get married. Come here, for goodness sake, let me hug you for once.'

Starting to cry Katy gave in and for a very unusual moment she accepted the caress, before backing off and wiping her eyes.

'At least you know now,' she said. 'I'll tell Gareth he can spread the news. He wants me to sit around and put my feet up but I've told him I'm going on riding for now, anyway.'

'But not Cass,' Patsy agreed with Gareth there. She was doubtful about Hedfa Aur but she remembered her own hot little horse in the distant days when she herself had been pregnant. She had been very unwilling to give up riding him and it had not done any harm but like Fly he had been

a known quantity. She felt emotional herself about the news but she knew that Katy would not appreciate any display of her feelings. She needed to carry on as normal.

There was good news on Patsy's answer phone as well. One of Hedfa Aur's mares from last season had foaled. It had been late in the season when he had covered the two mares, but a June foal would get plenty of sun and its mother good grass.

'It's a filly,' Patsy told her daughter later. 'Eleri is thrilled, it's her mare's first and she says it's a chestnut, flaxen mane and tail just like our boy. She wants me to go and see it.'

'You will, won't you?' asked Katy, and Patsy said that she would.

She decided to go the following morning, to see Highflyer's grand daughter while she was still new. The owner lived in South Pembrokeshire, the softer side of the county where the wild hills of the north gave way to a mixture of farmland and small towns, and also to many caravan sites and holiday attractions. The difference in atmosphere between the two parts of the county always took Patsy by surprise as the road off the hills flattened out and the houses took on a largely more suburban look.

Eleri Davis lived at a small tree nursery, specialising in ornamental fruit or garden trees, and the mare and foal were in a beautifully kept paddock with post and rail fences and a shelter. The mare was a cob herself, a nice-looking bay, and she came to meet them with her foal at her side. Patsy could feel herself smiling, enraptured, and Eleri, a lively youngish lady with curly black hair, laughed.

'Beautiful isn't she?' she said, and Patsy agreed.

The foal was her sire in miniature, a stocky, four square little horse with a curved neck and pricking ears, her foal coat already a strong chestnut with a fluffy flaxen mane and tail. Her head had the softer look of a filly but she was bold and curious, coming up to sniff and nibble at the visitor.

'She's gorgeous,' Patsy rubbed the little face and the mare reached out to check this person who was touching her baby. 'Have you thought of a name?'

'Well, this one is West Wind,' said Eleri, 'And your boy's name is Golden Flight in English isn't it? I thought perhaps Summer Breeze.'

'That's lovely,' agreed Patsy, secretly deciding that she would find the translation into Welsh to tell Emrys. It was crazy, but she still could not escape the feeling that, somewhere, he might still be interested.

The mare turned back to her grazing and the foal kicked up her heels and trotted ahead, showing off her springing cob trot.

'Come in for a coffee,' invited Eleri, and Patsy followed her in through a porch filled with young saplings in pots and unusual looking plants on shelves and into a cool, green and white kitchen.

There were photos on the light oak dresser, and Patsy immediately saw several of West Wind, some with Eleri on her back and others in hand at a show. Eleri switched the kettle on and came to stand beside Patsy.

'I used to show her quite a bit,' she said. 'But the nursery got busy and I started my own exotic plant part

as well as Greg's trees, so I decided on the foal.'
'Do you miss competing?' Patsy asked her, and Eleri said that she did.
'It always gives me a bit of a buzz,' she said. 'All the getting ready and the thrill of getting the best out of the horse in the ring. I hope I'll get back to it after the foal's weaned. Did you do much of it?'
'I did when I was young,' Patsy remembered Emerald, her sparky chestnut pony who would jump anything and who had taken her to pony club championships. She had adored that pony and even now the memory of his sudden death from colic left a sharp regret. There was always one, she thought, one who was special, as both David and Goliath had been, and Golly still was.
'These days I leave any of that to my daughter.'
Eleri laughed. 'You're lucky,' she said. 'I've got two boys and all they want to ride is motor bikes.'
She made the coffee and produced homemade cookies and Patsy tried not to feel inadequate. This lady seemed to have worked on many skills, her home looked perfectly kept, she was running her own soundingly ambitious plant business, her horse was beautifully kept and she planned to compete again. Patsy thought of her own comfortably lived in house, her healthy but somewhat disorganised horses, and her unambitious hacking and wondered if it was too late perhaps to push herself a little more. At least she had taken one new step with the trekking.
They drank the delicious coffee and Patsy ate two cookies before taking a final look at Summer and her

mother and setting off for home feeling obscurely restless.

It was raining the next morning, heavy, persistent rain which showed little hope of stopping. Katy helped her mother to bring the horses in to give them a break from it and Golly promptly lay down. Katy looked at him rather regretfully.

'I think jumping the other day left him a bit stiff,' she said. 'I need to get on with Fly, I'll ride him again tomorrow or he'll never be ready in time for the shows.' She hung up the head collars, pulled her jacket over her head, and headed for her cottage and computers. Patsy went into her own house, where even now, in June, the Rayburn was keeping the damp at bay, surrounded by cats. Katy getting restless again made her feel herself that the summer was passing, today was a reminder of how quickly it could go. She opened the drawer where she kept such things in search of schedules; it was already almost too late for the big show entries. The main local shows and the Royal Welsh all came close together in a few weeks in the height of summer. It was time to choose what to enter and get those entries in. The in-hand classes were not a problem with Gareth as handler but she was doubtful about Katy's plan to ride the stallion at the Royal Welsh. She knew, however, that her daughter was set on this plan and she filled in the entry for the ridden class and hoped that it would not prove a mistake.

The following day the sun was back and the breeze was soft. In the fields the grass seemed to have grown an inch overnight and it would not be long before it was time to cut it for hay. Katy brought Hedfa Aur in and fetched his tack.

The stallion had been ridden quite a bit the previous winter and had hacked round the lanes with Golly and he accepted being tacked up with only token resistance. They had decided that a quiet hack today would be a better start than going round in circles and Hedfa Aur strode out down the lane with arched neck and pricked ears, full of pride and ready for anything. Gareth, who had been at the farm helping his father with the lambs, was just driving home and Patsy saw his disapproving

expression and she wished that her daughter would stop trying to pretend that nothing need change. At least Fly, as Katy called him, behaved well. He knew that under saddle he had to accept control and although he was very interested when they passed some ponies in a field he let Katy remind him to behave and went on behind Golly, who was unimpressed by any of his companion's antics.

A neighbour, stopping his Land Rover as they passed, leaned out to admire him, and said 'You'll be winning everything on him this year. Under saddle, is it be, then?' and Katy said that it was.

'Have you entered him yet?' she asked her mother as the vehicle drew away.

'I have,' Patsy told her. 'But I really don't know that it was a good idea.'

'Because of my "delicate state",' Katy sounded defiant. 'I don't need to start putting my feet up yet. I'm sure I can make it past the Royal Welsh at least. What's first?'

'The Young Farmers Show,' Patsy told her. 'And the Royal Welsh and Cardigan.'

Katy looked satisfied.

'Great,' she said. 'I've always wanted a ride at the Royal Welsh, I'll just about have time before I have to turn into a blob.'

Back home she took the stallion into the school and went through the show ring routine, walk, trot, canter on either rein and some showing off movements including his spectacular trot. Gareth came out to watch and leaned on the gate without smiling. Katy was wearing her defiant look.

'It's good exercise,' she told him but Gareth looked unconvinced.

Cass was at his gate and Patsy thought that he looked a bit lost. She wondered if he had been used to more attention and she decided to bring him in for a brush and a break from his field. Katy had left her radio on the shelf and, remembering how he had seemed to react to music Patsy switched it on.

'Songs from the shows', she realised, as a Lloyd Webber number came on, and the pony pricked his ears to the sound of it. She began to brush him as the song ended and the music changed to something familiar with a lively, stronger beat. Cass's head came up and he pricked his ears and suddenly whinnied.

'What?' Patsy asked him. He was staring towards the door, head high, and Patsy stroked him, feeling the sudden tension leave his body as he realised that no-one was coming. Was it someone who brought a radio with them Patsy wondered, but surely if it was someone he bonded with like that they would not have abandoned him. It was a puzzle that they might never solve, she knew, as Cass went back to nosing some hay while she brushed the tangles out of his tail.

Gareth brought the collies over again, this time to work them quietly with Patsy's little group of sheep, getting them used to dogs, and watching him work the dogs Patsy thought how attractive he was, attractive and caring. Remembering her own fraught and rocky marriage she wondered if Katy had any idea how lucky she was.

The week before the show the weather turned hot. The skies were a clear, brilliant blue and the light had the dazzling clarity for which West Wales was famous. Katy worked on Hedfa Aur until he glowed and Gareth had given up trying to dissuade her. Watching her ride him in the school Patsy was suddenly consumed with envy. Eleri had stirred some ambition in her and as Katy headed for the gate Patsy made up her mind.

'Hold on,' she told her. 'Let me have a sit on him.'

'You?' Katy laughed. 'You only ride old Golly.'

'Time I tried something else then,' Patsy picked up her hat which she had left on the mounting block and Katy, looking bemused, got off the stallion and held his head.

Feeling the wide, muscular back under her and seeing the arched, shining neck in front Patsy wondered if she was mad but she was committed.

"I can do it," she told herself. "When I was Katy's age I

rode work on race horses, this one isn't half as sharp."
"But that was a long time ago," her sensible self reminded her, but Patsy ignored it. The stallion's ears turned back to check this new rider but she was familiar and when she squeezed his sides he moved off obediently. Patsy soon found that she was enjoying herself. Golly was familiar although even he could be a handful when something set him off, but riding the big moving, powerful cob was a different experience, thrilling and satisfying. She was so used to Golly that riding him felt almost as natural as walking but this took her back to the time when riding was an absorbing challenge.

She trotted, feeling the contained power in the big movement, and Katy called 'Go on then, give him a canter.'

Patsy did so and Hedfa Aur was strong but obedient. When Patsy got off she was laughing, exhilarated, and Katy stared at her.

'That's how you used to ride, when I was a kid,' she said. 'You can still do it.'

'Just,' Patsy knew that she would feel the effect tomorrow. 'I just need to get back in practise.'

'It looks as if you'll have the chance,' Katy sounded resentful. 'Seven months or so, if you all have your way.'

'It'll be worth it,' Patsy put her arm round her and for once Katy accepted it.

'I'm still scared, you know,' she admitted quietly. 'All this waiting, feeling things happening inside, I thought I wanted it, but suppose I can't cope.'

'Of course you will,' Patsy assured her. 'Everyone feels

like that, you'll be fine.'

'I suppose,' Katy pulled away. 'Here, I'll get his tack off. I've got the show to look forward to anyway.'

She led the stallion away towards his stable and Patsy felt that her daughter was at least starting to accept what was happening.

CHAPTER TEN.

The weather was still hot on the day of the show. The hills were a hard, bright line against the cloudless sky and the flies were out, bothering the horses so that they were glad to come in. Patsy decided to leave the ones to be left at home in for the day with a handful of hay each and Golly and the mare promptly lay down. Osbourne began to rub his itchy tail on the partition and Cass leaned his head over his door watching Katy polishing the stallion. Katy looked pale and admitted that she felt sick.

'It'll wear off,' she insisted. 'I feel like this most mornings now.'

Gareth was going to the show with them and Katy made a great show of feeling fine when he came to help them load. Hedfa Aur was quite willing to bounce his way up the ramp and Cass gave a shrill whinny, obviously complaining that he was being left behind.

The show was being held in three flat fields near the road, with separate entrances for cattle and sheep and for horses. Patsy found a parking spot in a quiet corner away from any obviously enticing in-hand mares or challenging stallions and Gareth and Katy, who had travelled in the groom's space at the back to keep an eye on the horse, got out. Katy looked almost green and Gareth concerned.

'I'm perfectly alright,' Patsy heard Katy telling him, and she determined to keep out of it.

'I'll get the numbers,' she told them and left them to deal with the horse while she went to find the secretary's tent.

It was a typical small agricultural show with horse classes for everything from jumping ponies to in-hand heavy horses. There were tents of produce and flowers and later there would be a parade of fox hounds. Fox hunting, although officially trail hunting these days, was still popular with the farmers who knew that the odd "mistake" when a fox was caught made one less predator after their lambs.

Patsy queued for the number and walked back to the lorry to find Hedfa Aur tied up outside with Gareth on guard while her daughter vomited into the hedge.

'She still reckons she's going to ride,' he told Patsy as Katy came back sheet white, wiping her mouth.

'I'll be alright,' she insisted, but Patsy decided to intervene.

'And if you aren't?' she asked, 'Are you going to get off and throw up in the ring?'

'So we just go home?' Katy was almost crying and Gareth put his arm round her. 'After all the work? Is this it, sit around and wait for all those months?' and Patsy suddenly knew what she was going to do.

'Of course not, this will pass,' she told Katy firmly. 'As for today, I'll ride the horse.'

'You?' Katy stared at her, suddenly looking better with the surprise. 'You haven't brought any clothes.'
'I'm still not much fatter than you, and we used to wear each other's clothes,' Patsy reminded her.
'Your boots will be a bit big but I'll manage, and l always keep a spare hat in the lorry.'
Gareth was looking disbelieving.
'Are you sure?' he asked. 'I mean...perhaps someone else would do it. I don't want to be rude, but..'
'I'm too decrepit,' retorted Patsy. 'I may not have done much for a time but I can still ride. If I can't cope I'll bring him out.'
A very doubtful Katy insisted on helping to saddle Hedfa Aur in his softly gleaming cob saddle and double bridle and Patsy hoped she would cope with the double reIns. Racehorses certainly didn't go in double bridles and neither had Golly and it was years since they had briefly owned a horse which did. Patsy got into the lorry and found that Katy's clothes were a tight fit, especially round the waist. The fastening would, she hoped, be hidden by the black show jacket and a spare boot strap would take the place of the button. Katy, insisting that she was recovering, resentfully pushed her mother's hair into a net and Patsy brushed her rather shabby spare hat.
'You don't look bad,' Katy admitted, regarding her critically. 'But I'm sure I'd be alright. Its's almost gone off now.'
'Too late,' Patsy decided to be brisk. 'They're calling the class.'
Gareth held the horse while she stepped onto the

stool they used as a mounting block and raised her foot into the stirrup. Hedfa Aur stiffened as she landed in the saddle, knowing that this was different, but Katy patted him and Patsy told Gareth to let him go.

'Be tough with him,' Katy instructed her, and Patsy nodded. She felt far from confident as the horse moved off, finding it hard to remember the last time she had ridden in a show, but they were on their way.

Hedfa Aur was very interested in it all, especially the other horses. There were some appetising looking mares and Patsy was careful to give them a wide berth. Passing rather close to another stallion brought a squeal but Patsy remembered Katy's advice and gave him a reminding tap down the shoulder with her whip.

There were not many entries in this class for Welsh cob stallions over four years. Many of the mainly stud horses were still at work or having a break before the big shows, and once in the ring Patsy found that she had plenty of room. Hedfa Aur recognised the command to behave and he did so, trotting and cantering round and taking up position in the line up without arguing. Engrossed in her horse Patsy's doubts left her and she found that she was enjoying herself.

"I can still do this," she realised. "And I've missed it."

They were called out one by one to do a short show, a figure of eight in canter and a full powered trot past the judges and Patsy felt the thrill of her horse's power.

Hedfa Aur's quality was outstanding in the fairly mediocre company and he won the class.

Riding out Patsy realised that he was receiving some disgruntled looks from the connections of other horses, and there were some comments in Welsh that she was glad not to quite understand. A Royal Welsh winner, even newly under saddle, was considered a bit too good for such a fun show, and Patsy realised that Katy had known that but had been determined to make the most of what she considered her last few weeks of freedom.

'That was great,' Katy sounded amazed when she met her mother and the preening stallion as they came away from the ring. She looked better now, almost back to normal.

'Professional,' was Gareth's comment, and Patsy grinned.

'Not quite decrepit then,' she said.

Back at the lorry she found that, in spite of the comments, there was still a high in winning.

'I'm alright now,' Katy sounded disgruntled. 'I could have ridden him.'

She was taking the saddle off and Gareth took it from her and got the brunt of her resentment as she pulled it back.

'I can manage,' she said. 'I don't need nannying.'

She thumped up into the lorry with the saddle and Gareth looked at Patsy.

'I thought she'd be pleased,' he said. 'She's so resentful, most women want to be cosseted.'

'She'll get used to it,' Patsy told him. 'I think the reality has only just got to her.'

She hoped she was right and when Katy got down from the lorry again she was glad to see her daughter grab Gareth's hand.

'Sorry,' she said. 'But it's deadly feeling helpless.'

'Hardly helpless,' Gareth kissed her, 'Just a bit of temporary weakness.'

'I think I could cope with a cup of tea now,' Katy told him. 'And maybe a Welsh cake.'

'I'll see to it,' Gareth told her.

He went off and Katy sighed. 'I must try not to blame him,' she said. 'I did agree to this, and it's taken long enough, but now it seems such a mountain ahead.'

'You just have to get used to it,' Patsy told her. 'You may not enjoy it but it's part of being female. You'd probably regret it one day if you didn't experience it, and just think of what you'll have at the end.'

'Dirty nappies and no sleep,' said Katy wryly. 'I can't wait.' She was quiet for a moment and then she suddenly smiled. 'And something like that.'

Looking round Patsy saw a young couple walking towards the ring, a very young baby in a sling against its mother's chest. Katy's expression had softened and Patsy said, 'That is what it's all about.'

'Oh, I know,' Katy sighed. 'Maybe one day I'll even be a pony owning Mum. That really might be fun.'

Gareth came back with tea and Welsh cakes for them all and pulled the folding chairs out of the lorry for them to eat in comfort. Hedfa Aur settled to his hay net and Patsy enjoyed the satisfied feeling of having succeeded in something.

The show went on around them, a succession of

horses done up to their best, of carefully washed and trimmed dogs bound for the dog show, and the people typical of all this, farmers in their good clothes, families with pushchairs and children, horse people in riding clothes and visitors to the area having a look at a local tradition. The background was a mixture of Welsh and English, chatter and commentary, and announcements about classes, lost children, and badly parked cars. It was all familiar and satisfying and Patsy had a sudden deep hope that whatever happened in the world this would not change.

Gareth's father had a pen of sheep in the agricultural part of the show and Gareth went off to see how they were doing. Eleri came by and congratulated Patsy on the showing class.

'I thought you didn't compete any more yourself,' she said and Patsy explained, making Katy squirm with embarrassment. Eleri laughed.

'Something similar happened to me once,' she said. 'At least you didn't get into the ring first. I had to abandon the horse and run for it.'

Patsy was glad to see Katy laugh but when Eleri, after reporting that the foal was fine, had gone she got restless and insisted on getting the stallion ready to load.

'I still feel like a prize cow,' she said. 'With everyone having a look at me.' and as soon as Gareth came back she had him load Hedfa Aur ready to go.

Patsy was driving carefully towards the gate when a rather shabby lorry caught her eye. There were two slightly moth-eaten looking donkeys, saddled and bridled, tied to it and something about the shape and the faded white stripe painted at an angle down the side touched a memory.

"That evening when the Shetland was dumped," she remembered. "I hardly saw it, but I'm pretty sure it was that lorry."

She stopped, reaching for her bag and a pen to take down the number, as a short, stocky man in cord trousers and a fleece jacket came round the side of the lorry accompanied by a skinny teenage boy. The ramp was down, hiding the number plate, and Patsy inched the lorry forward until she could see the number on the front. The donkeys were being untied and Patsy realised from the shabby tack that they must be giving donkey rides somewhere on the show ground. She scribbled the number down as in the back Hedfa Aur began to scrape, questioning why they had stopped, and Patsy moved on. It should be easy enough to trace the owner of the lorry if he was giving rides but what could she achieve? She had no proof that it was the lorry dumping a pony but she could ask around. It would make deciding what to do with him much easier if they could find where he might have come from.

The bay pony was at the gate as usual to watch when they drove in. He whinnied when he saw Katy and Patsy was again convinced that there was some mystery about his past that was more than just the dumping of an unwanted pony.

Cass galloped again that night. Patsy, getting ready for bed, heard him and went out again to watch. There was a moon, but it was waining, the dim light growing and fading as wisps of cloud sailed across the sky on a fresh breeze. Katy did not come out this time and Patsy hoped that she was curled up with a protective Gareth. The other horses joined in, stirred up by the strange light and the rising breeze, and Patsy watched as they ran in their groups, shining, unreal shapes more like horse spirits than solid four-legged creatures. Goliath, as the old spirit among them, was the first to stop and he joined Patsy by the gate to toss his head and snort until Osbourne also slowed up, leaving the mare and her son to run themselves out. Cass went on, still circling his small field, until Patsy called, when he finally stopped and stood snorting and steaming in the moonlight. Gradually they all began to graze again and Patsy, still intrigued by the mystery, found her slippered feet cold and went in to bed.

CHAPTER ELEVEN.

The next morning Patsy had to go to the local shop for milk and bread and when she got back she saw Everard Mackintosh leaning on the field gate feeding Osbourne on slices of carrot while his wife Tabitha looked on. Mack had some time ago lost the ponytail which had been part of him when Patsy first knew him and they were both a bit bronzed. Mack's greying hair was cut fairly short and there was a fringe of stubble round his chin. He was still an attractive looking man, his strongly boned face showing little sign of ageing.

Tabitha's sharp kitten's face was bright under her still dark hair and she was giving off a charge of suppressed energy. She had never seemed a peaceful person.

Osbourne was plainly glad to see his master and Patsy was surprised at how glad she was to see them. She had certainly missed her rides and chats with Mack but the sudden lift she felt at the sight of him startled her. He had been the first friend she had made when she arrived in Wales, he had shown her the safe ways round the moor on his big, black faced white horse, he was always easy to talk to, and had invited her to dinner and tried to deflect Tabitha when she tried to wind her up about her haunted farm house. He turned to smile at her now, his very blue eyes showing a warm welcome, and Patsy smiled back.

'Did you enjoy your cruise?' she asked them and Mack made a face.

'Tabs did,' he said. 'We saw a lot of old buildings and new markets full of too many tourists, like us, but it went on too long like some of those on board entertainments,'

'You fell asleep during a lot of them,' his wife told him, and Patsy laughed and asked them to stay for coffee.

Cass had come to his gate while they were talking and he was gazing away past them in his usual way. Tabitha nodded at him.

'Who's that?' she asked. 'New ride for Kate?' She always called Katy that. 'It looks fey.'

'What do you mean?' Patsy asked her, and Mack laughed.

'Take no notice,' he said. 'If it isn't ghosts it's fairies, anything to put some spice in life.'

'It looks far away,' Tabitha ignored her husband. 'As if it isn't really here.'

Patsy stared at her. Mack's wife had exactly put into words something that she felt about the bay pony. It was as if his mind was on something only he could see. She was about to say something about finding it when Katy's voice behind them said 'Hi everyone. Welcome back,' and Tabitha's attention changed to focus on her.

'Congratulations,' she said, 'Getting through the first three months are you?' and Katy glared.

'Trust Mum to spread the news,' she said.

'I haven't said a word,' Patsy told her, as Mack grinned.

'Fey, he said. 'Second sight or something. Do I take it that there is good news?'

'I suppose it's good,' Katy looked cross. 'If you call being sick every morning good news.'

'Tea, not much milk, plenty of sugar, before you get out of bed,' advised Tabitha, 'I'm told it works, it may not stop it but it won't feel quite so bad.'

'Thanks,' Katy sounded grudging and Patsy reminded the couple about coffee, and asked Katy if she felt like one.

'Urgh, not yet,' she said. 'I'm going for a walk down the wood before I have to do some work.'

She went off and Patsy asked 'how did you know?'

'Lucky guess really,' Tabitha told her. 'Queasy look about her face and softer look round her eyes.
I take it you're pleased, going to be a grandmother? It's a doubtful pleasure that I never had.'

There was something barbed in the way she said it, and in the look that she gave Mack, who took no noice but Patsy remembered Mack once saying regretfully that they had put off having children until it was too late.

'Yes, I think I'm more pleased than Katy at the moment,' said Patsy and Tabitha smiled her clever cat smile.

'Oh, she's pleased enough really, even just for proving

she can do it,' she said. 'She's certainly done something that I failed at. She's just a bit unsettled,' and Patsy realised that she was right.

It was a beautiful June day, the roses that scrambled over the old trellis at the back of the house were in full bloom and their scent filled the garden when they settled out there, Mack on the old wooden bench and Tabitha and Patsy on her old wicker garden chairs.

Patsy was not a really keen gardener but she kept the grass trimmed and pruned the roses. A grass covered stone bank separated the garden from the fields and there were ferns and patches of bright blue Speedwell among the grass. Mack, who said he enjoyed a spot of landscaping, had made Patsy a small pond in the corner and two goldfish were sunning themselves among the yellow flowers of a pond plant. Mack leaned back now, stretching his long legs in fawn linen trousers, and gave a satisfied sigh.

'It's good to be back,' he said sincerely and Patsy saw Tabitha frown.

'It's still benighted,' she said. 'After a few weeks of seeing some life.'

'Oh, I admit there were plenty of distractions,' there was an edge to Mack's voice. 'You certainly found them.'

'To use an outdated phrase, my dear, you were behaving like a stick in the mud,' Tabitha told him. 'Maybe,' Mack laughed. . 'But some of the people we met...'

He went off into a story about the Captain's table which Tabitha seemed to fInd less amusing, and she cut him short with a story of her own. Patsy realised that there was some tension between them, but soon she was laughing at Mack's tongue in cheek and Tabitha's enthusiastic stories of their cruise. Then Mack asked for more about the bay pony and Patsy told him the whole story.

'And I couldn't be sure but I thought I recognised the lorry that dumped the second pony,' she said. 'It seemed to belong to a man giving donkey rides at the show.'

'Aled Williams,' said Mack at once. 'Been towing those asses round the country for years. Dumping a pony though, doesn't sound like him, if he wanted rid of it he'd be more likely to turn to the local glue factory and get a few pounds.'

'Mack's right there,' agreed Tabitha. 'He certainly isn't a man to miss a sale.'

'Is he local?' asked Patsy. 'Maybe he was just after some free grazing.'

'He's from the other side, Milford way,' Mack told her. 'I don't know how much land he's got. Maybe someone was paying him for keep and he decided it didn't need to be on his own land.'

'I wonder if I could find out,' Patsy got up to pour more coffee. 'I'm sure there's some story behind it.'

'Doubt if he'd tell you anything,' said Tabitha. 'He's one of the old school of Welshmen, they find it hard to talk to women, especially English ones. I asked him his donkey's names once and you'd think I was going to curse him.'

'You were wearing your cape that day,' Mack told her. 'I expect he thought you were a witch. She has that effect on people,' he added to Patsy, and she was surprised to catch a hint of malice in his voice. They all laughed but Patsy knew there was some truth in it. There really was something witchy about Tabitha.

Coffee over they went back outside and Mack looked at his horse, grazing alongside Goldie.

'I suppose the old boy had better come home,' he said. 'He's going to miss the company.'

'Eithin Aur will miss him too,' Patsy told him. 'There's no rush if you want him to stay for a bit. I was planning to put the pony out with her when Osborne goes but I'm not sure they'd settle.'

'I'd like that,' said Mack. 'While we see if we can settle back to life in the sticks. I've missed things here but I can't say that for my wife.'

He surprised her with a quick hug, gave the horse another carrot and they went off, leaving Patsy feeling flattered. Did Mack mean that she was one of the things he had missed?

Would it be worth finding Aled Williams and trying to sort out Cass's story she wondered later. It would be good to know the pony's history. She might as well try.

It was not hard to trace Aled Williams and his donkeys. Computers were not Patsy's thing but she could cope with an iPad and next day when she tried tapping in the name and donkey rides it brought up an address in south Pembrokeshire and a rather clumsily written advertisement for donkey rIdes as entertainment for fetes and children's parties. When she mentioned it to Katy her daughter was not in a mood to be enthusiastic. She was in the middle of working out a complicated web site for a client.

'By the time my stomach settles enough for me to look at a screen I want to get some work done,' she told Patsy. 'Then I might get time for a ride while I still can. Tabitha's cups of tea don't seem to be much help.'

She was cross and frustrated but Patsy knew that all she could do was leave her to it. She decided to go in search of Aled Williams on her own.

It was a beautiful drive over the top of the Preselis with the road climbing through the open moorland. Once over the cattle grid the land dropped away on the right and beyond it the craggy tops of Carningli, the angel mountain, rose up against the brilliant blue sky. The distant sea was on three sides up here and as the road reached the crest the southern view of it also came into view and Patsy pulled into the wide lay by for a few minutes to enjoy the feeling of being on top of the world. Two red kites were swinging and hovering, riding the warm up-currents, and sheep were everywhere, newly shorn and very white among the bushes and the rough grass. It was quiet and green and ageless up there but Patsy made herself turn back onto the road and drive on down into the flatter farmland of the south.

To get to Milford the road crossed the Cleddau bridge over the estuary and it was soon after that Patsy saw the turning that she had found on the map and a couple of miles further on as houses grew closer together and the country more urban she saw the gate to a small bungalow and the donkeys grazing in a field at the side. There was room to pull off the road by the gate and Patsy got out. At the sound of the latch the donkeys looked up and a ragged black and white collie slid round the corner of the bungalow and came to meet her followed by the scrawny teenager that Patsy had seen at the show.

'Is Mr. Williams about?' Patsy asked him.

'Himself is down the field back there,' the boy told her. 'Is there something you want?'

'It's about donkey rides,' Patsy improvised. 'For a child's party.'

'You'd best come round and see him,' the boy aimed a slap at the dog who was sniffing doubtfully round Patsy's legs and it swerved away. Patsy followed him round the side of the bungalow and saw a line of sheds and beyond them a couple of fields, quite well kept, and the man from the show working on one of the fences. There were several horses grazing, all looking quite healthy but elderly, with dipped backs and patient faces. The boy shouted and the man left his roll of fence tape and came to see her.

'Lady about donkey rides,' the boy told him and the man surveyed her. He had pale blue eyes and a closed expression and Patsy remembered Tabitha's remarks about his attitudes to English women.

"Like Emrys,' she thought, remembering her "ghost's" reaction to her when she had arrived at Bryn Uchaf.

She told her story about considering donkey rides for her grandchild's birthday and he briefly gave her a price. Hunting desperately to find a way to ask questions she turned to look at the horses.

'They look like old faithfuls,' she said. 'I've got an old boy, not quite retired yet. Have you had them a long time?'

'When were you after the asses then?' Aled Williams was certainly not interested in conversation.

Patsy hastily pulled a date out of her mind and he said he would go inside and check his book. He went towards the house, followed by the collie, and Patsy was left with the boy, who was staring at her.

'I seen you at Clinden show,' he said. 'You was riding that classy cob what won the saddled class.'

'That's right,' agreed Patsy. 'Do you ride these horses?'

'Not them,' the boy sounded scornful. 'They're just people's old rubbish, Himself takes them in when folk are too soft to send them to Robinson's, they'll pay him to keep them alive and not have the bother themselves.'

Robinson's, Patsy knew, was the local knacker.

'Does Mr. Williams have many like that?' Patsy asked him, and the boy suddenly looked cagey.

'Not here,' he said. 'That cob you were on, that weren't old.'

It was clearly a change of subject and Patsy, hearing the house door close, knew that it was all she was going to get.

Aled Williams said the donkey date was free and Patsy said that she would let him know. He nodded and turned to the boy.

'I'll get back to my work then,' he said over his shoulder to Patsy. 'Come on Ethan.'

It was quite clearly a dismissal and Patsy thanked him and went to the gate, shepherded by the collie. She felt sure that her suspicions were right, Aled Williams had dumped Cass, but she was no closer to finding where the pony had come from.

CHAPTER TWELVE.

But you must know where he went,' Simon was frustrated. Sylva's pony, her beloved Spotlight,
whom she had persuaded him to buy for her when they saw him in dire condition at the sales.
She had nursed him back to health, and focussed all her love on him when their father walked out, he couldn't be gone out of reach. Spotlight had been his rather strange twin's main hold on life after that desertion and their actress mother's scant attention. He had been another part of it before that misguided business with Drake had made her cut him out. Marg, to whom he was talking, looked defensive.
'I didn't want to have the pony put down,' she said. 'I know how fond of him Sylva was, there was something special between the two of them. One of my clients had sent her lame pony to a small sanctuary, they just asked for a donation. She said it looked alright on a video, man had donkeys as well. I thought at least Sylva could be honestly told Spotlight hadn't been a put down and your mother agreed to it.'
"She would," thought Simon. He knew that their

mother could no longer face what had happened to her daughter. She had escaped from it back to her long-standing job as a character in a well-known tv soap and an apparently humane way to solve the pony problem would have been more than welcome.

'Where is this sanctuary?' he asked Marg, and she found the address for him. It was in West Wales, an area he didn't know, but he decided to visit it. He could at least make sure that Sylvia's pony was alright. It was Saturday next day, he would go then.

The journey proved to be to a dead end. When Simon, who had not driven so far since passing his test, finally reached the destination that Marg had given him he found a derelict farm. It was a jungle of nettles and brambles growing over collapsed buildings and walls and when he enquired at the nearest pub he was told that it had been deserted for years and that there was a doubt over who owned the property. With a horrible sinking feeling Simon knew that Marg had been conned and that Sylva's pony was almost certainly dead.

CHAPTER THIRTEEN.

There was a small herd of ponies crossing the mountain road as Patsy drove home. She stopped to watch as they made their way on down the rough land towards the small farm in the fold of the hills.

There were several foals with them and the masterful little bay stallion was keeping the group together. He was all pride and possession and Patsy wondered how Hedfa Aur would manage a herd of his own. Cob stallions did not get the chance to run wild like these Welsh section As, they were too big and civilised and potentially dangerous.

"I'd like another foal on my place", thought Patsy. "It's a bit late in the season but l could still have Goldie covered, especially now that Katy won't be able to ride her for much longer."

She suggested the idea to her daughter later and Katy looked cross.

'It hasn't happened yet,' she said. 'I can still ride. Suppose we put Goldie out of commission and something happens? I'd be stuck horseless then.'

'Nothing will happen,' Patsy told her. 'Even less risk if

you take a bit of sensible care. Riding that dodgy mare isn't the best idea anyway, if you want a ride you can get on Golly.'

'And I can ride Fly here,' Katy sounded stubborn. 'There's the Royal to come don't forget.'

'I haven't,' Patsy could see trouble ahead over that plan but she would not mention it yet.

'Let's plan for later,' she said now. 'Another foal would be fun. Perhaps not another cob, something with a bit of quality that you can bring on when your own offspring is growing up. What about putting Goldie to a thoroughbred?'

'Yes,' Katy liked the idea. 'I'll look around online.'

Katy searched online and found a likely stallion not far away.

'He's not pure bred, part Irish,' she said. 'But he was a useful eventer and several of his foals have turned into decent competition horses.'

'He sounds right,' Patsy studied the photos. 'Jacaranda, by Jaccando. Let's go and have a look, we don't want to waste time, it'll be a late foal anyway.'

'He's grey,' Katy was still studying the photo. 'I'd like a grey.'

They went next day, Katy willing to take a morning off after her stomach had time to settle. The horse was at a yard near Newport and the drive took them through winding green lanes and out onto a different part of the hills with wide views down over the farmland to the sweep of Cardigan bay. The small fields formed the patchwork pattern that was a feature of Pembrokeshire, fenced by hedges and stone walls and dotted by white cottages and compact small farms. The weather was blue and white and the breeze enough to dot the blue of the sea with white wave crests. Katy leaned back, silently drinking it in, and Patsy left her to it, glad that her daughter seemed to be finding some inner peace.

The yard was tucked into a spot where the road began to drop down out of the hills. A tidy black and white board read 'Hillcrest Sport Horses.' The drive was crushed stone leading to a traditional stone farmhouse a bit larger than Patsy's with a wide porch and wide glass doors facing the view.

Two terriers ran to meet them as they got out and woman with curly blond hair and dressed in jeans and yellow tee shirt came round the corner to meet them. 'Angie Farr,' she said. 'You've come to see Jac.'

Patsy agreed that they had and the woman led the way round the house into a smart yard edged on two sides by loose boxes and on the other sides by a fence and gate into a school and on the fourth side by the wall of a large barn from which, surprisingly, came the sound of music.

Several heads were looking out over green painted stable doors, one of them grey and imperious, and Angie Farr said, 'Typical Jac, he always has to see whose arrived.'

She took a supple brown leather head collar down from a hook by the door and the grey backed up politely to let her into the stable. Patsy and Katy went to the door to look and Angie said 'Alright to come in, he's very civilised.'

The horse was impressive, a dappled grey with a dark mane and tail and all the quality of a thoroughbred with a little extra bone from an Irish ancestor. Katy held out her hand and the horse sniffed it and lipped it with gently inquiring lips, and Angie asked if they would like to see him out.

Out in the yard the horse looked just as attractive and he walked away and trotted back with an easy swinging stride.

'Your mare's a cob, you said?' asked Angie.

'Yes,' Patsy told her. 'She's bred one foal, Hedfa Aur, he was champion at the Royal Welsh last year.'

'I remember him.' Angie looked impressed. 'But you aren't after another cob?'

'We're hoping to get a competition horse,' Patsy told her. 'I don't really breed, Hedfa Aur was pure chance, the mare was in foal when I bought her.'

'Has this one done any competing?' Katy asked her, as Angie turned Jacaranda back towards his stable, and his owner said 'Oh yes, dressage recently, but he competed up to advanced eventing. There's one of his sons working in the school now, he's a part bred out of a Connemara mare.'

She took the stallion's head collar off and shut his door. 'Come and have a look.'

She led the way round to the end of the barn like building which turned out to be an indoor school.

The music was coming from inside and Patsy and Katy followed Angie in through the door into a small gallery with a row of chairs on a platform overlooking the arena. There was a grey horse working in there, cantering very slowly in time with a lilting piece of music. As they watched the tempo changed into a longer flow and the horse's stride lengthened with it.

'This is Jack the Lad,' Angie told them. 'Julie bred him from her mare, he's six now.'

'He's just the sort I'd like,' Katy told her, and Patsy said 'He's lovely. I thought riding to music like that was just for big warmbloods. I've seen it on television.'

'Any horse can do it,' said Angie. 'It's getting quite popular. The horses seem to like it, they get to know their own music.'

The music changed to a lively beat as the horse came back to a trot and turned up the centre line to come to a halt just after the music stopped. His rider patted him and smiled at Angie.

'Just behind it again,' she said. 'He got a bit forward in that lengthened canter and we were late to trot.'

It sounded like a different language to Patsy but she got the idea. It had been lovely to watch and the idea of having a horse schooled to do it was very attractive. Katy was slightly less impressed.

'I want something that will jump,' she said. 'I've never been very keen on dressage although it looks nice.'

'Jack jumps as well, doesn't he?' Angie appealed to Jack's rider, who brought her little horse over to them.

'He's great,' she said. 'Ten preliminary points eventing. He'll have a go at most things, like most part Connies.'

'And Welsh cobs,' added Angie, as she went to open a

wider door nearby to let Julie ride out.
Angie took them into her pleasant, sprawling farmhouse kitchen for coffee and they discussed her stud fee. Jacaranda did not run with mares but Angie assured them that he was an experienced stallion and that her husband helped to handle the covering.
They agreed a provisional date and Patsy and Katy set off for home over the heat shimmered hills.
For a time Katy was silent, gazing out at the view, the window open and the breeze tossing her hair.
Then she looked at her mother.
'It makes me sort of believe in a future, of being back to normal and working a horse like that,' she said. 'We will send Goldie, won't we? The two of us can be broody together.'
They took Goldie over to the stallion a couple of days later. She was immediately interested, sniffing the air and lifting her top lip, and Angie laughed.
'I don't think this one will take too long,' she said, and Goldie tossed her head and called, immediately at attention as the stallion answered. She would stay there until it seemed likely that she was bred. Patsy and Katy drove hopefully home.
There were more visitors wanting to ride next day, fairly experienced teenage girls. Patsy set out for the moors with them, Cinders and Sweep in their usual order behind Golly, who was getting used to these treks and becoming resigned to the fact that they would be slow and boring, unlike his gallops over the high tracks with Mack and Osbourne.
It was a typical Preseli day, bright, warm sunshine

with sudden sharp shining showers sweeping over the hills. Patsy decided to risk the slightly challenging circuit up the first steep slope round a large area of bracken and down the rough, sunken track which would take them back to the causeway along the edge of the bog. The causeway had been built as access to a lonely farm, set high on the slope under the shelter of the hill. It was long deserted, just the stoney banks dividing the fields and a few collapsed walls remaining, a stronghold of wildlife. There were rabbits in the banks, a badger sett, and once Patsy seen a polecat vanish down a hole with a rabbit in its mouth.

They cantered here, beside the bank, the little group of horses starting keen but the ponies running short of breath before they reached the top. The girls enjoyed it, laughing and patting the ponies and exclaiming about the view, some of the lower land veiled for a few moments as another silvery shower swept through.

There were wild ponies up here, the usual group with the grey stallion, and Patsy saw that the dumped Shetland was still with them as part of the herd. There would be a distinctive non-native foal out there next spring.

The stallion was used to ridden horses, he kept his mare's apart and watched as they slithered down the steep sunken path back towards the flatter land and the gate. They were making their way back to the causeway when Patsy saw another pony coming towards them in the distance across the bog and she knew that they could have a problem. It was this

time of year that the moorland stallions drove any colts who were starting to be a challenge out of their herds, sending them off to find mares of their own, and occasionally they would start to be a nuisance. This one was coming at full speed, jumping the tiny streams and plunging through the heather, obviously set on trouble. It was a creamy colour, a bright spot of colour against the dull brown and green of the boggy land, and the girls were exclaiming with pleasure at the sight. Patsy knew that she had to warn them.
'He's pretty, isn't he,' she agreed. 'But he may be a bit too interested in us, Cinders especially.'
'Because she's a mare,' the grey pony's rider understood.
The colt was coming up fast, swinging to turn in behind them and squealing a challenge. Cinders pricked her ears, trying to look round, and Patsy said 'ride her on firmly and you Haley try to get Sweep alongside. I'll see if I can make him back off.'
She held Golly back, turning to face the colt, brandishing her stick at him and shouting a threat, but he tried to dodge. Golly flattened his ears and snapped at him but the colt was determined. Sweep's rider had managed to persuade him alongside the mare and Patsy turned Golly to go up on the other side. The colt circled them, trying to get close to Cinders. He dived at her from behind, neck stretched and head low in an immature copy of stallion behaviour and Cinders, annoyed now, kicked at him. Her rider was getting anxious and Patsy said 'The gate's straight ahead. Kick her on towards it, Hayley, go with her. Golly and I will

keep him back.'

The two girls did as she said and Patsy turned Golly to ride him off. The old horse was only too willing to help. He was irritated by the colt's persistence and when Patsy rode him at it waving her stick, he flattened his ears and ran at it. Startled the colt swung away, back into the rough ground, and with Golly's help Patsy kept it there as the two girls headed for the gate. Patsy waited, glancing round until she saw Haley jump off to open it, and then she turned Golly to follow them. The colt came along behind for a few yards and then decided that it was no use and as it turned away Patsy let the impatient Golly gallop to join them.

To Patsy's relief the girls were exhilarated by the adventure and Patsy praised them for their sensible riding. It could have been much worse, she knew, ending with someone falling off or getting kicked. She was thankful for the way her old horse had grasped the situation and helped.

When she heard about the incident Katy said Gareth would tell his father and get whichever of the graziers owned the colt to take it in. The mountain was part of the National Park and any animal that could pose a threat should be moved. Riding a mare out there was always slightly chancy but the mature stallions were usually no threat so long as riders did not cut them off from their mares.

The fields seemed very empty with Goldie away. Hedfa Aur was restless, circling his field and watching for his mother to come back although Golly was peacefully grazing. Cass caught the restlessness and hung about by his gate. Katy, coming out for a break from work, went to talk to him while Patsy swept out the lorry.

'Music,' she said over her shoulder to Patsy. 'Remember he seemed to be trotting round when my radio was on? What if he really was, perhaps he's done dressage to music at some time.'

'It's possible,' Patsy leaned on her broom to think. 'Can you remember what it was
playing that time?'

'Some traditional stuff, I think,' said Katy. 'Green sleeves, Strawberry fair, things like that.'

I've got an old disk of that kind,' Patsy told her.

'Let's try it,' Katy looked animated. 'I'll get him ready.'

'I thought you weren't going to ride the dodgy ones,' said Patsy, but Katy said 'He's been fine here, and I won't carry a stick. You find that tape and your old player. Let's see what happens.'

Patsy closed and bolted the lorry ramp and went into the house. It was very warm outside but with the Rayburn out the house was cool and silent. Patsy missed the stove in summer when it made the house too hot but with it out it felt as if something was missing, a murmuring central point like a living creature. Telling herself not to be fanciful she went upstairs to the spare room to find the old player.

Trying it, she got no response and she realised that the batteries would have died long ago. There were some in the kitchen drawer and by the time she had changed them and got back

Katy was riding the bay pony in the school. Cass was trotting, looking a bit tense, and Patsy slotted the tape into place and switched it on.

It was lively music, updated traditional tunes played by a group, and Cass seemed to react at once. His ears went forward, he dropped his nose and accepted the bit, and his trot stride became more regular. When the rhythm changed to something more lyrical he seemed to lose his balance for a moment and Katy asked him to canter. It seemed that she was right, cantering Cass regained his balance and they circled the school twice before the music changed again to something fast and jerky and the pony faltered and his head came up. Patsy switched it off and Katy brought the pony to the gate.

'I'm sure he's done that before,' she said. 'Worked to music. He felt quite different for a bit.'

She patted Cass, who was staring out across the yard, and who now whinnied before swinging restlessly round. Katy patted him and he swung his head to nuzzle her foot.

'I'm sure he's missing someone,' she said. 'It would be good to find out who it is. I'll give him a canter round before I bring him in.'

Cass seemed to accept that nothing had changed and Patsy watched him go off round the field. There was some history there she was sure.

CHAPTER FOURTEEN.

Sylva was restless, moving her head on the pillow, and the doctor who had been called in to check her said that she was very near the surface.

'It needs something, something to reach her, and she might come out of it,' he said. 'I don't want to try medication, ask the brother next time he comes in if there's anything that might help, music, maybe. Most kids of her age have favourite stuff.'

The nurse agreed to try it.

'Music?' Simon thought about the nurse's question on his next visit. 'She was quite keen on country and western, that open roads and long trails stuff, I could bring something. And of course there was her dressage music, something we arranged together for her and the pony using my keyboard.'

'That's a new one to me,' the nurse told him, and Simon explained.

'It's what she used to do with her pony,' he said. 'Riding at different paces to music. She worked out the floor plan and the movements, like choreography, and I worked out the music. They did pretty well in competitions.'

He brought the disk with him next day and put it on. The first notes were designed to accompany the horse into the arena and to the first halt and after a pause long enough for a salute a bright tune took the test into trot. Sylva, who had been lying still and unresponsive in her usual way, suddenly stiffened and Simon held his breath. Her hands, lying relaxed on the sheet, closed into loose fists and her wrists curled a little. Her eyelids were fluttering and her lips moved as the nurse slipped softly out of the room to find the doctor.

'Syl,' Simon said quietly. 'Now, canter to E, change the rein...' The rhythm of the music changed and he tried to remember what came next. She seemed to be away now, her hands moving and her head turning on the pillow, and as the doctor came quietly into the room the final strong notes brought the test to a final halt. There was a moment's silence while everyone held their breath. It seemed impossible that Syl would not open her eyes. Simon found himself silently praying but then his sisters face crumpled and there were tears seeping into her hair and she seemed to withdraw back into her lost state. The doctor, nodding to the nurse to check her blood pressure, sighed.

'There's something blocking her,' he said. 'Something she doesn't want to face.'

'To do with that pony,' said Simon. Looking at his sister's still face he wondered how, if she was ever able to hear him, he would be able to tell her what he suspected was the truth.

CHAPTER FIFTEEN.

'Mum, Mum, look,' Patsy came out of the stable at Katy's shout and they both stared, amazed, as the bay pony in the field changed smoothly from canter to trot, turned down the field, and came to a sudden halt facing the gate.

'That was weird,' said Katy. 'He looked as if he was doing a test...'

The pony stood for a moment and then suddenly his ears went back, he snorted, tucking his tail in, and dived forward.

'He's crazy,' exclaimed Katy, as Cass shot off down his field. 'What is it with him?'

She and Patsy watched as the pony swung round the bottom of his field, slowing to a trot, and stopping to shake his head. He snorted again, shook himself, and whinnied, before relaxing, lowering his head, and starting once more to graze. Katy shivered.

'I reckon it's your ghost,' she said. 'He looks haunted.'

'I don't think Emrys was into dressage,' said Patsy. 'But I know what you mean.'

She remembered Tabitha saying that the pony looked

as if his mind wasn't really here, and her own feeling of his mind being on something else. Horses were telepathic, she was sure of that, they did react to other horses and to people when there was no obvious connection. A top dressage horse could seem uncannily sensitive to its rider's signals and horses often knew that their owners were approaching long before they could see or hear them. She herself had known that split second when her horse knew she intended to canter or take a certain path before she consciously knew it herself. Could the sense work over a long distance, though, if someone they knew was thinking about them hard? And if such a thing was possible why would such a horse have been dumped?
'We really have to try to find where he came from,' she said now. 'I've got a feeling that it might be important.'
'That man you went to see, the donkey man, he must know,' said Katy.
'But he certainly isn't going to tell me,' Patsy pointed out. 'But that boy who works for him, he must know something. I'd have to get him alone, though.'
'Find out where he's giving donkey rides next,' suggested Katy. 'I bet he'll be at Cardigan show in a couple of weeks. I'll look up the schedule.'
She went off and Patsy stayed, leaning on the gate and wondering if some sort of telepathy could really be at work.
Katy reported that there actually were donkey rides among the entertainments at Cardigan agricultural show. Hedfa Aur was entered and so she would have

the chance to try again to find out about the dumping, but before that there was the Royal Welsh.

When Gareth realised that Katy was planning to ride Hedfa Aur at the Royal Welsh there was a blazing row and Katy slammed furiously round to her mother's.

'He says I can't ride,' she declared. 'It isn't fair, he can't tell me what to do, I've told him other women go on much longer, even jumping, but he says riding Fly in a class like that when he could be a handful isn't on. He says the baby's his as well as mine and he's got some say in it.'

'He has got a point,' Patsy thought that Gareth was right. 'It is a risk, it'll be hectic in that main ring.'

'So we withdraw,' Katy was bristling, and Patsy made up her mind.

'I'll ride him,' she said. 'I enjoyed the Y.F.C. show, it'd be a thrill in my old age.'

'You'd need new clothes,' Katy was finding herself backed into a corner, but she was not going to admit that it was a sort of relief. Patsy recognised that and found that she was suddenly excited. It gave Katy an honourable way out and it would be a great experience.

'Then I'll get some,' she said. 'The farmer's co-op in Cardigan has a good riding department, and I can borrow your jacket again, I just need breeches and a hat.'

Katy gave in, crossly.

'I might have known you'd side with him,' she said. 'Don't blame me if Fly carts you. I'd better come shopping with you, make sure you don't get carried away by anything too fancy. You'd better get a jacket as well if you're set on this, they'll all be ultra smart.'

It was decided. When she had gone Patsy did have doubts but she was committed now.

Mack laughed when he came to ride Osbourne and she told him.

'Good for you,' he said. 'I'll be there to watch.'

'Won't Tabs be bored?' Patsy did not want to cause resentment, but Mack shrugged.

'I doubt she'll come,' he said. 'She'll say it's too Welsh or something, but I'm sure she'll find something else to do.'

'Mack...' Patsy hesitated and Mack turned back to finish saddling his horse.

'Come on,' he said. 'Let's take these two old lads round the Hafod, if you're up for a gallop.'

Patsy decided that she was. If there was a problem between Mack and his wife it was not her business to probe.

CHAPTER SIXTEEN.

At her livery yard near Cardiff Marg was watching as a girl who sometimes came to use her school worked her horse. It was a nice little grey part bred Arab and she was riding to music from a player balanced on the mounting block in the corner. The music brought them up the centre line and ended with a closing crescendo as the horse halted a few strides too late, its head coming up as it hollowed at the sudden tightening of the reins.

'I'm still not getting it right,' the girl sounded frustrated. 'That weird pony of the half-witted blond girl never seemed to have any trouble.'

'Sylva isn't half witted, just a bit different,' Marg told her. 'She and her pony had an unusual understanding.' She still felt guilty at the memory of what she had done about Syl's pony but she had not been given much choice. Probably Spotlight was safe anyway in the man's sanctuary, at least he would not cause another accident.

'Is she alright now?' Nikki sounded a bit odd, looking down to tidy her horse's mane. 'I...well, I think Drake and I upset her. She went off in quite a tantrum, really laying into that pony with the end of the reins.'

'When was this?' Marg was suspicious, and Nikki looked truculent.

'I don't really remember,' she said. 'We were riding together and he'd...well, he'd got his hand on my knee and Sylva came up on that pony and got all silly and said she thought he was going to ride with her and tried to push between us. Drake said something about not wanting to ride with a child and...and we both laughed and she just lost it. Drake got angry then, shouted at her and waved his stick at the pony and she laid into it with the end of her reins and went galloping off.'

'So that's what caused the accident,' Marg was furious. 'And neither of you had the guts to explain. You let us all blame that pony. You knew how anyone hitting it made it panic. No wonder Drake moved his horses.'

Should she tell Simon, she wondered? He was sure to want to accuse Drake, who could turn nasty and there was nothing he could do now. The pony was gone and Syl was still unconscious.

CHAPTER SEVENTEEN.

Patsy fetched Eithin Aur back from the stud, delighted to learn that she was was probably in foal. She would have her scanned as soon as possible but first there was the Royal Welsh.

It seemed that the whole of Wales went to the Royal Welsh. Shops closed for the week, farming families worked on a rota for essential jobs, teenagers begged or borrowed caravans in which they could sleep between parties and for whole families it was their annual holiday. The rest of the country seemed suddenly deserted and every road led to Builth. They all seemed to be on her road, too, thought Patsy, as as she drove her old lorry, with Gareth and Katy in the back with the horse, in the dawn line of show bound traffic over the narrow bridge and round the edge of the old town, following the signs to the horse box park. In the back Hedfa Aur whinnied as they made the turn in and Patsy knew that he would have his head up, peering through his small window at the familiar sight of a show ground.

They were lucky enough to find a parking spot on the

edge of the slope down to the main show ground. As always the sight sent a shiver of awe down Patsy's back. This was what Wales was all about, the celebration of its life, of its main industry of farming, its history and its traditions. The view was of a sea of tents and stands, of flags and bunting, of roads between the trade and display avenues, and of the green rings where champions would be made.

There were horses being unloaded everywhere and a little further on the overnight stables buzzed with activity. Surveying it all and feeling the building tension around as classes began Patsy felt her own nerves tense. She must be mad plunging into this on her still inexperienced little horse
after so long as a spectator but it was too late to change her mind. She was committed and Katy would be scornful for ever if she pulled out.

Hedfa Aur was excited, staring round, shining with bursting health and spirits. Katy brushed and polished him and supervised her mother's preparations while Gareth guarded the horse. Looking at herself in the shabby full-length mirror which Katy kept in the lorry Patsy felt disoriented. It was an unfamiliar reflection that she saw, the close fitting black jacket with the velvet collar over the white show shirt, her face done by Katy with a touch of makeup, her still mainly dark hair back in a neat bun under the new black velvet covered hat.

'You look pretty good,' Katy told her. 'For goodness sake don't let him rub his head on you and mind any mud before you get on.'

The class always had a huge entry and the preliminary judging took place first in an outside ring. Katy held the horse while Patsy climbed carefully on board and gathered up the supple, shining reins in her dark gloved hands.

'Gareth will walk down with you,' Katy told her. 'And I'll come in when they strip. Good luck, it's going to take a long time.'

Hedfa Aur bounced his way down the walkway from the boxes to the ring with Gareth's steadying influence at his side and then Patsy was on her own, circling the huge outside ring as one of a mass of gleaming, rounded, crested cobs all with full pride and instincts but mostly amazingly calm in
the sea of horses.

There were over ninety entries and they were divided into groups for judging, performance first and then conformation. Walk, trot and canter one group at a time and then individual shows, done two at a time at different ends of the ring. Hedfa Aur was excited and strong and Patsy found her arms aching and her hands sore in spite of the gloves but she managed to keep him in position and he was calmer in the individual show. She could not help being relieved when it was time for conformation and she could dismount and stand at his head while Katy unsaddled him for the judge's inspection.

'You're doing alright Mum,' Katy told her. 'Some of them are all over the place.'

Hedfa Aur, used to being shown in hand, ran up well and at last it was time to re-mount and wait, for ever, it seemed, for the numbers to be announced for the final judging which would come later in the main ring.

They had got through. Patsy felt a rush of satisfaction as she rode out, she had done it, proved she still could ride, and not let anyone, Katy, or crazily Emrys, down. It was time to return to the box for a break and a tidy up before the final judging.

It was growing hot now, the sun beating down on the green bowl in the hills that was the show ground, and it was going to be even hotter in the main ring. Hedfa Aur, who had thought it was all over, was reluctant to set out again, tidied up and with Patsy starting to feel sore in the saddle, but he accepted it.

This final was a different experience altogether. Riding into the huge, green ring with the tiers of packed stands and the surrounding streets of displays Patsy felt intimidated. She was not an experienced show rider as were most of the other competitors although Hedfa Aur did not seem to be worried. He had been in the main ring before, of course, in hand, when he won the Prince of Wales cup, and he liked showing off. Patsy had a job to restrain him as the final qualifiers circled the ring and they were called in as one of the final ten to give their individual display.

Hedfa Aur was more than ready, he had done enough standing about for one day and he refused to settle to trot and led off wrong for the canter. By the time he did start to concentrate Patsy knew that it was going to be too late, this class was finally judged on performance. She was not surprised when two other cobs were called in before there was a short pause and then the steward beckoned her forward. Third. Hardly a disgrace but she could not help feeling disappointed as they made the lap of honour in the wake of the surging applause for the winner.

They were all waiting when she left the ring, Katy and Gareth and Mack. Patsy was suddenly aware of feeling exhausted. Her legs ached, her head ached, her hands were sore and she did not think she had ever been so hot in her life.

'Well done Mum,' Katy did not look too disappointed and Gareth took hold of the stallion's bridle.

'Let your Mum get off,' he said. 'I'll walk the horse back, she looks as though she's had enough.'

'Thanks,' Patsy could hardly wait to get out of her hat and the close-fitting jacket. She slid carefully out of the saddle as Hedfa Aur tossed his head, impatient to get back to his lorry, and someone steadied her as her legs almost gave way.

'You look as if you need a drink,' it was Mack with his arm round her waist. 'Here, this'll do as a start.'

He put a thankfully cold bottle of water into her hand as Gareth led the stallion away and Katy looked back at her, suddenly grinning.

'See you in a minute Mum,' she said. 'Looks like you've got a carear.'

Patsy was pulling her hat off, her hair sticking to her head and round her face as the hairnet came off with it and Mack helped her out of her coat and watched as she drank.

'That was nice riding,' he said. 'I'm impressed. You did

really well.'

'I wasn't that good,' Patsy finished drinking and undid the neck of her show shirt. 'Katy could have won it. That other cob wasn't as good quality as Fly, it was my display that lost it.'

'You can't know that,' Mack told her. 'So far as I could tell you did a great job. Come on, if you can make it back to the lorry I'll hunt up a proper drink.'

He kept a friendly arm round her shoulders as they walked back up the long hill to the lorry and in spite of the heat Patsy was glad of it.

"I thought I was pretty fit," she told herself. "I shouldn't feel like jelly."

It had been a very long class, though, and the heat in that valley was extreme. Back at the lorry Katy and Gareth were washing Hedfa Aur down while he tugged happily at his hay net and Patsy dropped thankfully into one of their folding chairs in the shade from the lorry. Mack looked at her.

'What's it to be?' he asked. 'Coffee or brandy? Or something long and cold?'

'Coke,' Patsy told him. 'There's some in the cold box. Katy...'

'Leave it to me,' Mack sounded gallant and Katy grinned at her mother as he got into the lorry.

'Always thought he fancied you,' she said. 'If he wasn't stuck with that witchy Tabitha.'

'Katy...' Patsy began, but Mack was coming back with the welcome drink, and she stopped. It was nonsense, she and Mack had always been friends.

With Hedfa Aur washed and cooling off Patsy drank

her coke and leaned back in the shade feeling satisfied. She had done it, ridden a good horse in the main ring at the Royal Welsh, something a short time ago she had not dreamed of doing. It had been a thrilling, exhausting experience, and successful enough to be satisfying. Perhaps she need not leave all life enhancing efforts to her daughter after all. She was tired driving home but it had been worth it.

CHAPTER EIGHTEEN.

The summer weather was holding fair and it was more than time get the hay in. Two days later Patsy walked across to her back field, closed off while the grass grew. It was up to her knees now, the earlier brilliant green softened by the heavy seed heads gently browning under the midsummer sun. Gareth had already put some of his work on hold to help with his father's hay and he would bring the tractor and cutter round to Patsy next.

This was always a twitchy time for everyone with hay to cut, it was already late in the season after the earlier less settled weather, a heavy shower at the wrong time could spoil a season's crop and anything more than a shower could mean complete ruin. All the farmers had their phones tuned to the met office and their own instincts on fine alert. The first early crops of silage were cut and the hay cut for haylage wrapped but that was less sensitive to getting wet. It could still keep in its wrappings, but dry hay had to be dry when cut. If it got wet it would mean must and mould in the unwrapped bales which were best for most horses.

Glad that she did not get hay fever Patsy stopped in the grass to breathe it's sweetness and watch the shining ripples from the slight breeze. There were rabbits grazing on the shorter grass on the headlands and the warm air was alive with the voices of wood pigeons and the mewing of a buzzard family. In the distance she could hear the clatter of the baler on John and Rhianne's farm next door and she knew that it would not be long before the cutter arrived.

Gareth started cutting that afternoon. The hay fell in shining sheaves and Patsy leaned on the gate watching with Katy. The horses too were interested at first but they soon accepted the clatter and the enveloping sweetness that drowned out any other scents. The cut hay looked perfect but Patsy knew that she would be on tenterhooks over the next four or five days waiting for any chance of rain to spoil all the weeks of growing.

The next two days were perfect. Gareth brought the rake over and turned it so that it lay in fluffy lines. This was its most vulnerable time, when rain would penetrate right through it, and the met office forecast was hinting at more changeable weather on the way.

'It's pretty dry,' Gareth announced. 'It should be right for baling tomorrow if I leave time for any dew to dry.'

By evening, however, it was clear that it would be a near thing. The pressure was dropping and there would be an increasing risk of thunderstorms but when Patsy looked out of her window first thing next morning the sky was still clear. Outside it was getting hot and the flies, often a sign of approaching storms, were bad and she brought all four horses into the stable. Cass was restless but Golly lay thankfully down in his shady box. He hated flies which always seemed attracted by his white patches.

Gareth was there with the baler by late morning and in the sky the first few white clouds were beginning to take the threatening shape of thunder heads.

'I'll have to help carry them,' Katy announced as the first bales rolled off the machine. 'We can load them into the horse box, it's the quickest way. We can't leave carrying until Gareth finishes, look at the sky.'

'Not you,' Patsy told her. 'That would be risky.'

'You can't do it yourself,' Katy told her, and Patsy knew that it was true. They would have to wait for Gareth. She was ready to argue with Katy when there was a clatter of tyres over the cattle grid and Mack drove in.

'Thought you might need help,' he told them cheerfully, and behind his back Patsy saw her daughter laughing

Patsy was gratefully thanking him when a Land Rover pick up arrived and Rhianne got out dressed for working in jeans, loose top, and gloves, and accompanied by Gareth's father. The rescue party was complete.

The job took them the rest of the day with Patsy driving the horse box between field and barn, Katy with her mother's pick up, and Mac and Rhianne and John loading as Gareth drove up and down the cut lines with the baler. They worked faster and faster as the sky darkened and the bales piled up and with the last

one done Gareth jumped out of the tractor and came to help.
Behind the hills the thunder rolled and Mack grinned. 'Here it comes,' he said. 'We'll just do it.'
He was right. As the first huge drops hit the dusty yard the last bales were rolled out of the lorry and he and Gareth carried them inside. A vivid fork of lightning shot across the black sky and the rain was suddenly a torrent, roaring on the tin roofs and making the horses, even Golly, jump and shy.
Katy shot back to close the pick up's windows and dived back already soaked. For a few minutes they stayed, watching the downpour, Gareth with his arm round Katy, brushing the dripping hair back from her face, until Patsy said, 'I've got some cider in the old pantry, it'll be nice and cool. Shall we run for it?'
There was general agreement and they piled into the house wet and laughing. Patsy went to the cool stone pantry for the cider and Katy collected glasses and varied crisps and biscuits for snacks and the gathering rapidly became a party. The cats perched disapprovingly on the Rayburn, cold and unlit at the moment, and everyone sprawled on Patsy's comfortable old chairs, discussing the hay crop and the weather and moving on to local gossip. Soon Mack was bringing out his cigarettes and. asked Patsy if she minded if he went outside for a smoke.
Patsy did not mind, she knew that Mack was an incurable smoker, he had even been known to go down a line of jumps on a mock hunt with a cigarette between his lips although he did now limit his smoking

to out of doors. Katy put a tape in Patsy's ancient player and a Lloyd Webber song began to form a familiar background.

The storm was moving away and Patsy, still finding it hard to convince herself that they had really succeeded in beating it, slipped quietly out to make sure that her precious hay was really out of danger from flooding or a leaking roof. She was standing gloating over it and it's sweet scent from the barn door when Mack, having finished his cigarette, joined her and put an arm round her shoulders.

"All is gathered safely in," he quoted. 'Well done.'

'Thanks to all the help,' Patsy reached up to give him a friendly 'thank you' kiss on the side of his cheek and Mack turned her to face him.

'It was a pleasure,' he said quietly. 'Patsy...' his very blue eyes were searching and his kiss was gentle at first but on her mouth and as she hesitated, too startled to react, it become firmer, tasting of cigarette and cider, and his body was strong and still youthful. Her long quiet instincts took over so that she found herself with her arms round his neck kissing him back with unexpected ardour. When he stopped kissing and smiled down at her Patsy stared at him, feeling dazed and slightly unsteady.

'I've wanted to do that for so long,' he told her. 'Watching you ride, all happy and free with your hair coming out of your hat and the wind in your face, and here, lively as a girl, with your lovely shape in your sensible clothes, and now, seeing you all fulfilled with your luscious hay crop. You don't mind, do you? Don't say you're shocked or something.'

'No...' Patsy regained her voice. 'No, I don't think you could call it shocked. Mack, I just never guessed...we've been good friends, but...'

'I hope I haven't spoiled that,' he looked anxious and Patsy found that she wanted to reassure him.

'No,' she was unable to resist reaching up to touch his face. 'I...I knew I missed you when you were away...and now I think I know why. But Tabs...'

'Has an interest of her own,' Mack's voice was bitter, and Patsy stared at him.

'You mean...someone?' she asked, and Mack said, 'yes...someone from that cruise that she'd met before. It's been coming for a long time, don't go thinking I'm just on the rebound.'

'I...I see.' Patsy felt out of her depth. 'Mack, we ought to go in, perhaps...'

'We might see what happens,' Mack gave her another, much lighter, kiss. 'Come on then, back to the fray.'

He took her hand to lead her back into the now light rain and Patsy let him hold it for a minute before she pulled away. This was so utterly unexpected she did not know what to think.

She had been content as she was with her home and animals and her daughter, and a few good friends, did she really want this sort of disturbance? Confusingly her body told her that perhaps she did.

Katy was drinking orange juice and she was alert enough to give her mother a close look as Mack followed her in, but it was not until later, when everyone had gone home and Gareth was driving the tractor and baler back that she said anything.

'So what were you and Mack up to out there?' she asked. 'No Tabby cat around today. I said he fancied you.'

'I don't know what you mean,' Patsy told her, but Katy laughed.

'Of course you do,' she said. 'You were all flushed and soft and that old boy looked as if he'd found some cream.'

'Nonsense,' Patsy knew that it was inevitable that Katy would suspect but she wasn't going to tell her daughter what had happened. To Katy Mack was just that, an old man, and any pleasure that she had felt with him would seem weird. She firmly changed the subject and Katy let her do so. It was something about which she needed a lot of time to think.

CHAPTER NINETEEN.

The weather settled now after the heat and the storm into typical summer weather, warm blue days alternating with warm, wet windy westerlies when winds from the Atlantic brought sweeping downpours across the country. Two days before Cardigan show, one of the more settled days Rhianne rang to ask if she could take two more trekkers.
'Experienced teenagers,' she said. 'They asked me to say they'd like to go up to the top if you can manage it.'
'I'll check them in the paddock first,' Patsy told her. 'But the weather looks good enough if they are.'
She went to fetch the ponies in and it was when they reached the yard she realised that she had a problem, Sweep had lost a shoe. He would probably manage a short ride round the flat area but if she did what they had asked and took them up to the Golden Road along the top it was rougher going and he would soon be sore.
'Golly,' thought Patsy. 'If they're any good one of them

could ride him and I'll ride...what, Goldie or Cass?'
She had ridden Eithin Aur but the mare was unpredictable, although Katy enjoyed trying to out think her, Cass was still an unknown quantity but apart from apparently being scared of whips he had done nothing wrong. If the girls seemed competent she would ride him. She put Sweep in his stable and went to catch the bay pony.

Instead of being two girls as she had expected the teenagers turned out to be boys, about thirteen and fifteen.

'Our Aunt's got horses,' the older one, Brian, told her. 'She jumps them a bit. They're not rocking horses.'

'We don't want a lesson,' the younger one, Chas, added, but Patsy insisted on seeing them in the paddock first. They were typical boy riders, fairly balanced and able to control their mounts, but impatient at the confines of the school and Patsy had a few misgivings. She wished that Katy could come but as well as being supposedly off riding she had gone to see a lady in Carmarthen who wanted a web site developed. She couldn't send these two away now or it could earn Rhianne's holiday business a black mark. She fetched Cass and mounted him and led the way out, leaving Sweep calling indignantly after his friend.

The boys, as she had suspected would happen, were not content with trekking speed. Patsy kept it to a trot along the causeway, Cass seeming a bit surprised by the whole expedition and Golly wearing his hard done by face because of his strange and less balanced than usual rider. It was a sultry day with the sun out but a hint of mist in the air and Patsy vowed to make the time high up as short as possible.

As the stony causeway gave way to grass the boys demanded to canter and Patsy, knowing that the slope would soon slow them down, agreed.

'Stay behind me,' she told them, but Golly was used to galloping up the hill and Cinders followed him. They soon passed Patsy's unfit pony and Patsy stood in her stirrups and urged him on.

As she had hoped the steep climb soon brought Cinders back to a walk and Golly, knowing the ride, dropped back as well. By the time Cass puffed his way up to them the boys were circling back to meet her.

'That was great,' Brian was grinning and Chas was patting Cinders. 'Can we canter again?'

'In a bit,' Patsy told him. 'We've a bit more climbing to do first.'

By the time they reached the top where the old drover's road led past rocky outcrops and on towards the southern lowlands the horses were all blowing and there was white lather on Cass's neck. Pulling up to tell her riders about the view Patsy realised that it was rapidly vanishing as one of the Preseli mists came down. They were not far from the rather faint path which led back downhill and Patsy risked trotting on until she saw the rock that marked the way.

Golly knew that they were going home. He was looking resentful again and Patsy knew that if annoyed he could decide to be difficult. Telling Brian to keep him close behind her she turned Cass down the path.

The bay pony was less used to the hills, the scrambles and slithers of the ways and the way the light and the mists changed it all. He hesitated, trying to test the ground, and Golly lost his patience. He pushed past Patsy's pony and was off down the path, swallowed up quickly by the mist, and Patsy called, 'Slow him up, wait,' as she grabbed the grey pony's bridle to prevent her from following.

She heard Brian shout 'whoa,' and Golly's clattering descent and Cass began to go anxiously sideways.

'Can you keep her back?' Patsy asked Chas, who said rather nervously that he thought so. Patsy closed her legs firmly on Cass and the pony gave in and they continued the scrambling descent.

The mist was thicker, the damp gathering in shining drops in manes and tails and making the humid air seem hard to breathe. Patsy heard a distant shout through the mist ahead and remembered anxiously that the path below turned sharply right to skirt the edge of the boggy land at the bottom and as they came out below the mist she saw that what she had feared had happened. Golly had gone straight ahead and he was now floundering in the thick bog with Brian desperately trying to urge him forward.

Few of the bogs out here were deep enough to drown a horse but the wet mud was thick and holding and Golly was not making much progress.

'Get off him,' she shouted. 'Try to lead him...your weight is making it harder.'

'I'll sink, I might drown,' the boy sounded scared and Patsy said 'you won't, it isn't that deep, just sticky.'

Beside her on Cinders Chas looked scared as well and Cass was swinging round, alarmed by the sense of panic. Brian had scrambled off landing up to his knees in the thinner surface water, but Golly seemed to be giving up.

'Chas, you get off too,' Patsy told him. 'You'll have to hold these two while I try to help Golly.'

Looking relieved to be on firm ground the boy did as she said and Patsy put Cass's reins into his hand. 'Just don't let go,' she said, and Chas nodded. Looking for the firmest spot Patsy stepped into the mud.

Brian was still holding Golly as Patsy reached them but she could see that her old horse had decided that he was there to stay. Even when Patsy struggled round behind him and slapped him he gave no more than a token heave and he seemed to be sinking deeper. Patsy was suddenly really scared, was it definitely not possible to drown in the mud? She knew that she must get help.

Katy and Gareth were both working away, she tried Rhianne's number but it went to answer 'phone. That left Mack.

Mack answered at once and was immediately practical.

'I'll need your quad,' he told her. 'And some rope. Don't let him struggle, he'll just dig himself in deeper. Be as fast as I can girl, stay calm'

He rang off and Patsy, feeling wet mud seeping over her boots and seeing Golly's nose drooping to touch it, all the same felt warmly reassured. Mack would cope.

Even down low now the mist was thick and wet, and the two ponies were getting restless. Patsy sent Brian scrambling out of the bog to help his brother hold them while she stayed by her old horse, rubbing his ears, and talking to him softly. The mist muffled everything but in a surprisingly short time Patsy heard the roar of the quad bike coming closer and it loomed out of the mist with Mack standing on the foot rests riding it in full 'hero to the rescue' mode.

It was soon clear that Mack had done this before. He plunged through the mud to the horse, rope over his shoulder, and with him directing her Patsy helped him to get the ropes round his bottom and back to the bike.

'Stand clear,' he instructed, and very slowly the bike began to move and the rope tightened. Feeling the pressure Golly decided that he was no longer about to die and made a valiant plunge forward.

Moments later he was on firm ground, plastered in dripping black mud but standing on all four feet. The boys cheered and Mack stopped the bike and came to unfasten the ropes.

'Looks O.K.' he said, and Patsy shakily thanked him. Mack put an arm round her shoulders and gave her a hug,

'I'm always here when needed,' he said, and Patsy managed to laugh.

Mack offered to walk back with Golly but Patsy would not abandon him. Chas got back on Cinders and Brian, also dripping with mud, walked with Cass while Mack drove slowly ahead on the bike.

By the time they reached home Golly was exhausted. The thick mud was plastered halfway up his sides and his tail was a black, dripping rope. Patsy was not much of an improvement, the mud had begun to dry inside her boots and it was thickly splattered all over her, and neither Brian or Mack was much better.

'Hose for the lot of us,' stated Mack. 'Then I'll run these two back to the farm and be back to help you clean up the old boy.'

The boys, recovered now from the scare, thought it a great idea. This far from the hill the sun was out, reflecting off the wall of mist which hid the high ground, and it was warm. Mack made a great game of hosing everyone down before loading the soaking pair into his very nice car to be driven to their, hopefully, not too horrified parents.

'Back shortly,' he told Patsy. 'Just chuck a rug over the old boy for now and sort yourself out.'

It seemed sensible to do as he said. Patsy hauled off her soaked and muddy boots and breeches and by the time Mack returned she was outside again in dry jeans and wellies starting to hose Golly.

Mack was still muddy but he had been wearing strong boots and work trousers and he had suffered less from the bog. He gave her a quick kiss and took the hose from her and she sank gratefully onto
a bale of wood chips.

There were some cuts on Golly's legs from sharp bits of stone in the bog and when most of the mud was off him Patsy found her antibacterial spray and treated them with it.

'I'll get the vet to have a look at him,' she told Mack. 'He still looks pretty done in.'

The ponies and Cass were out in their fields but Patsy decided to leave Golly in for a time. She gave him a hay net but as soon as she closed his door he lay down gratefully. Looking at him Patsy felt guilty. She should never have put Brian on him, she knew that her old horse could sometimes take matters into his own hooves. She could have let the boys ride the ponies in the school and the field instead. There was one good thing though, Cass had proved that he could be useful, if he was here to stay he need not be a burden.

The vet promised to come in a hour or so and Mack said that he would wait.

'You get properly cleaned up, I'll shout if the vet comes before you're ready,' he said, and Patsy agreed. She left Mack settled in her chair by the Rayburn, looking thoroughly at home with a cup of coffee and a cat on his knee, and went to soak off the last of the mud in the bath. Perhaps these treks were going to prove more trouble than they were worth.

The vet, an elderly man, found nothing seriously wrong with Golly although one of the cuts was quite deep. He gave him an antibiotic and left Patsy some sachets of Bute in case he was stiff next day.

'His heart's fine,' he said. 'But he's not young, like us. He'll probably feel the effect for a week or so.'

He drove off and Patsy went indoors to report to Mack, who was dozing with the cat by the stove. Pausing for a moment to look at him Patsy knew that the vet was right, they were all growing older, although she did not often feel it. Mack, she saw now, had more lines on his face than he had when she first knew him although his tanned skin still looked tight and the shorter hair suited him. He really was quite tasteful, she realised, and found herself smiling. Mack opened his eyes and saw her looking at him.

'Good news then?' he asked and Patsy told him. Mack tipped the cat off his knees and got up.

'He'll be fine then,' he said. 'He's tough, like us.'

He put his arms round her and kissed her, taking longer this time, and Patsy let herself relax and enjoy it. There was certainly nothing old about him now, he was an excellent kisser, but there was a warning in her mind. She mustn't start taking this seriously. Mack let her go and looked at her.

'I'll be away for a couple of weeks,' he said. 'Agent to see and a book fair to show up at as a promotion...and my solicitor. I'm not expecting Tabs to be here when I get back.'

'Mack, I'm sorry,' Patsy told him. 'Are you going to be alright?' Mack kissed her again.

'I'm hoping so,' he said. 'If you need an escort horse while I'm away use Osbourne, and Patsy, keep thinking about me. We aren't too old to try something new.'

He went out of the door, the cat running out in front of him, and Patsy was left in her empty room feeling as if her whole perspective had suddenly changed.

Katy was concerned when Patsy told her about the trek.

'Poor old Golly,' she said. 'He always did get himself

into trouble when he decided to take over. Remember that mock hunt when he wouldn't wait and jumped into a field of pigs?'

Patsy remembered it well. 'I still don't know who got the biggest shock,' she said. 'Golly or the pigs. It was a good thing today, though, Mack being able to haul him out.'

'I bet he enjoyed it,' said Katy. 'Rescuing the damsel in distress. I hope you thanked him properly, and not just with a cup of coffee.'

'Katy...' Patsy tried to sound dismissive but Katy saw through her.

'Why not?' she asked. 'If it wasn't for the witchy wife I bet you two could make a go of it.'

'Actually that might change. Tabitha is leaving him,' Patsy told her. 'Would it bother you, if I let something happen between us?'

Katy stared at her.

'I knew he fancied you,' she said. 'Good on you Mum, if the witch is out of the way and you want to go for it. He's a nice old guy. You don't want a lonely old age, just, well, be sure about it.'

'He's the same age as me,' Patsy did not feel old age creeping up yet. 'And anyway I'm not expecting anything long term. Just a bit of company.'

But Katy's words made a mark. If anything did come of it she must be sure that it was really what she wanted.

Golly was stiff the next day and his leg was swollen. It was a nice day and Patsy turned him out and was glad to see him roll and then wander off to graze. Rhianne had two more prospective trekkers due for her next week and thanks to Mack's offer of his horse she would be able to take them. Cass had been good but it was not sensible to rely on him when she knew he was not really hers to use as well as the doubt about his past behaviour. Perhaps she could find something out about that at the show.

CHAPTER TWENTY.

It was Cardigan agricultural show next day. For once show day was fine. Cardigan Show, held as it was at an often stormy time of year, was not famous for good weather. By tactical agreement Hedfa Aur was being shown in hand with Gareth handling him.
The cob classes, always popular, were in the middle of the day and by the time Patsy drove Hedfa Aur, loudly shouting his arrival, into the horse lorry park, the day was hot and the show crowded. Katy, coming back from checking which would be their ring, reported that Aled Williams, his boy, and the donkeys were doing a brisk trade at the far end of the field. Patsy decided to try her investigation at once.
Leaving her daughter and Gareth putting the final polish on the stallion she went to find them.
It was not easy to get the boy alone. He was doing most of the leading, helped by an enthusiastic young girl with dark hair in a plait and dressed in shorts and a tee shirt. Aled himself was taking the money, organising the queue, and lifting children on and off with

the regulation permission of their parents. Patsy had to wait for the donkeys to be given a rest while their owner went off to the refreshment tent and the girl was sent to the burger stall for food for herself and the boy before she went over to stroke the donkeys. They were eating their own lunch out of nose bags, long ears flapping as they concentrated, and they took no notice of her. Patsy looked round and realised that the boy had recognised her.

'Wasn't you the lady what came round about a party?' he asked her. 'Aled said you wanted something else, thought you was welfare for animals or something.'

'I'm nothing like that,' Patsy told him. 'But there was something else. Do you remember a bay pony with a white mark on his neck? I think Mr. Williams collected him from somewhere.'

'I dunno,' the boy looked evasive. 'There's some come and go.'

The girl arrived back with the burgers and handed him one, and Patsy asked her the same question.

'There was one like that in the old shed one day when I came round,' she said. 'Mr Williams was cross when he saw me looking and told me I was nosey. It weren't there again.'

'So neither of you know where it might have come from?' Patsy asked, and they shook their heads but Patsy noticed the boy's hesitation.

'Those burgers smell good,' she said, 'I wonder if those fresh doughnuts over there are as good?'

She fished some pound coins out of her pocket and he caught on at once.

'He did talk to someone on the phone,' he told her. 'That old lorry wouldn't start and he said as how he'd be late collecting their pony and asked if he had to turn at Pencoed. There was a new pony around next day but he went off with it again round tea time.'

'I hope those doughnuts taste as good as they smell,' Patsy handed him the coins. 'Thanks.'

She saw the first of the in-hand cob stallions coming up the walkway from the lorry park and went to watch. It seemed as if she was on the right lines but it wasn't much help.

Hedfa Aur enjoyed being shown. He had a natural 'look at me' presence but he did not let it spoil his manners. Patsy had seen most of his rivals before but there was one newcomer, a black horse with huge natural action even in walk. Unusually it was being shown by a woman and Patsy could see that it might offer some real competition for her horse, although it's manners were not as good as Hedfa Aur's as it jogged and tugged at the stallion bit in its mouth. After a couple of circuits of the ring the judge called them into line in no special order and the individual judging began.

There were classes in the other sections of the huge ring marked by cones, palominos in hand in one and coloured horses in another.

Hedfa Aur stood out impressively for the judge, Gareth smart and efficient at his head, while in line the black horse pawed and fidgeted. Patsy found Katy at her side as her stallion trotted up with all the fire and impressive action that had made him a winner before and Katy said, 'he still looks like a winner but will the judge like the new boy as a change?'

'Not unless it settles down,' said Patsy as the black horse came forward. 'I wouldn't like to try to run it up.'

The judge stood aside and waved the horse on to trot and they set off. The leader was trying to establish a long rein to give the horse a chance to show his action but as they turned to trot back

an over excited palomino in the next ring stood on end and the black cob lunged hard sideways. His handler was knocked off her feet, and the next moment he was loose and off round the ring at a full, pounding trot looking for trouble. He went through the palomino ring scattering them in all directions and swung back to the other cobs who were turning round and snorting. Hedfa Aur was on the end of the row and as the black cob came alongside, neck and head stretched and tail up in challenge, he swung to face it. Gareth was barged sideways and the two horses faced up to each other, squealing and striking. The other competitors were heading for the exit as Gareth and the woman handler tried to intervene. Gareth caught Hedfa Aur's reins but the other horse was wading in and he was knocked sideways. The whole thing had escalated in seconds and as the two horses began to fight in earnest Katy was suddenly gone, heading for the scene before Patsy could stop her.

In the ring Gareth had managed to grab the rein again and one of the stewards and the woman handler had

the black cob's reins and the two enraged horses were dragged apart. Katy had reached them and as Gareth stumbled, obviously with a damaged leg, she took over Hedfa Aur. Patsy joined her as she came out of the ring hanging onto the prancing stallion with Gareth limping behind.
'Give him to me,' Patsy told her. 'He'll have you over.'
'Is he hurt?' Katy was looking at the horse's legs but he seemed alright, and Patsy took the horse from her daughter as Gareth joined them looking white and angry, and grabbed Katy's arm.
'You promised not to take risks,' he told her. 'You should have left us to it,' and Katy pulled away.
'So I leave him to break a leg,' she retorted. 'You let him get loose.'
She was about to flounce off after the horse when Patsy noticed the blood in a rip in Gareth's trouser leg as Hedfa Aur swung round her.
'You're bleeding,' she told him. 'You'd better get that looked at.'
Katy turned round, suddenly concerned. With the black horse banished from the ring the other competitors were being called back in and Patsy knew that it was up to her.
'You'll have to retire him,' Katy told her, but there was someone on the other side of the stallion and the boy with the donkeys said 'want a hand Mrs?'
'Can you manage?' Patsy asked him but the boy's hand on the rein seemed confident and he said 'Mr. Williams has all sorts in, I'll help.'
Hedfa Aur, very full of himself after his fight, pranced

in between them and Patsy was glad of the boy's help. The judges had already made up their minds and they did not keep the remaining competitors waiting. Hedfa Aur was first and the steward waived the trot round as the horses were upset and the class running late.

Outside the ring the boy accompanied her back to the lorry and Katy arrived back to help reporting that Gareth's leg needed a stitch. Patsy unhooked the showy, three tier rosette and handed it to her helper.

'I wouldn't have got this if you hadn't come in with me,' she said, and the boy beamed.

'It's great,' he said. 'It can go with my footie sash over my bed. Thanks Mrs.'

'Call me Patsy,' she told him and the boy nodded and went to stroke the stallion, now tied up securely by Katy.

'I saw something else next day after that pony you was asking about went,' he said. 'There was this smart halter thing in the shed, it had a shiny brass bit on it with a name, Spotlight.'

So Cass had a name. Patsy thanked the boy and he went off, carrying the rosette proudly, and Katy looked a bit annoyed.

'That was a good rosette,' she said, but Patsy was unrepentant.

'We'll still have the card,' she said. 'And the prize money. That boy deserved it, he got Fly back into the ring with me and now we've got a name for the pony. It really might help to trace him.'

'I suppose so, if we must.' Katy started to sponge

Hedfa Aur down. 'Spotlight, I suppose those two white bits do stand out if it's sunny.'

'Or moonlight,' Patsy remembered Cass galloping in the night and the illusion of the white patch as a hand on his neck. She felt a sudden frisson as she once used to do when there was some sign of Emrys's presence. There had to be more to Cass...Spotlight's ...history than just that of an unwanted pony.

'Even if you find where he came from what's the point?' Katy asked. 'He must have been dumped because no one wanted him. Why would they want him back?'

'But we've no legal right to him,' Patsy told her. 'If he stays we need to get him a passport and a microchip, I don't want to be accused of theft by finding and keeping. The best way to do that would be by tracing his owner.'

Katy had left Gareth having his leg patched up, and said that his mother was with him.

'She was over by the sheep pens watching,' she said 'She and Gareth both had a go at me for risking going to help. That's why I left them to it.'

'They're just anxious about you,' Patsy told her, but Katy scowled.

'I just wish everyone would treat me as usual,' she said. 'I shall start thinking I'm fragile myself if you don't all drop it. I just want to forget about the wretched baby until it arrives.'

Gareth hobbled back leaning on his father's sheep crook and accompanied by Rhianne and Gareth said that his leg was sore but nothing was broken.

'Let's get the boy home then,' said Patsy.
Hedfa Aur went cheerfully into the lorry, undisturbed by the day's adventures, and Rhianne said that she would drive Gareth home to save him from having to scramble into the lorry. Katy said that she would keep Patsy company, gave Gareth a quick kiss, and climbed in beside her mother.
'I do love him,' she said. 'But he is a bit smothering at the moment. It did take a long time for me to get pregnant, I know he was scared it would turn out to be his fault, but he wouldn't think of any tests and I certainly didn't want to go there.'
She leaned forward to wave to some friends and Patsy concentrated on driving, feeling that quite a lot had just been explained.
At home Cass, or Spotlight as now seemed likely to be his name, watched eagerly as the stallion was unloaded and Katy went to speak to him. He nuzzled her but as usual he seemed to be looking beyond her for someone else and Patsy sighed. If he really was looking for the someone who had arranged to dump him she was afraid that they would never come.
There was another trek for visitors of Rhianne's the following day. Katy, working at home today, watched rather doubtfully as Patsy saddled Mack's big horse. Cass had been no trouble on the last eventful trek but there still had to be a doubt about him and Osbourne seemed the safer choice as escort.
Osbourne was kind and obliging but much bigger. The cobs were about fourteen two and Golly fifteen hands but Osbourne was sixteen three, great for Mack's long

legs but a long way up for Patsy. She and had ridden him once when out with Mack and knew that he could be strong and he was used to his owner's very casual and confident style of riding.

'You'll look like a midget on him,' Katy told her. 'I just hope you don't have to get off and get back on again out there.'

'I'll find a rock or something if I do,' Patsy told her, but her daughter certainly had a point.

The trekkers were two youngish women whose husbands had gone for a day's sea fishing. They were competent riders and Patsy knew that it was a good day for her to try escorting on Mack's horse.

It was a struggle to reach down to open the gate onto the moor but Osbourne was obliging and waited until she managed it. He was, however, used to Mack's habit of going straight off again at canter and Patsy had to haul him back. The ladies laughed at his hard done-by expression and one of them said that she had never seen such a strange coloured horse.

'He'd be almost albino without that black head,' she said. 'He's really a one off.'

"A bit like his owner," Patsy thought, as she patted him and tried to copy Mack's long reined and utterly relaxed style of riding.

They cantered properly a little further on when the sheep fields near the gate were left behind and Patsy felt her spirit lift as it always did as the great green and brown expanse spread around them. The heather was turning purple now, it's colour deep amid the patches of gold, sheep nibbled furze and the skylarks spiralled up from it. Recently shorn sheep bounced away at the thud of hooves and two foals leaped up, startled, from their sleep in a hollow and ran to their calmly waiting mothers.

Osbourne's stride was long and fluent and after the choppier stride of the cobs Patsy was reminded of the racehorses she had once ridden. Perhaps it was time to be more ambitious about a horse for herself. She was aware of a feeling of waking, of wanting things that she had more or less abandoned, the challenge and satisfaction she had felt in the show ring, the flowing, forward feeling of a quality horse and perhaps something more deeply personal, something she had never thought to feel again but which was bringing her more fully alive. As she pulled the big horse up and the ponies came alongside with their laughing riders she knew that she was hoping that Mack would not be away too long.

Golly was not looking much better. He looked rough and dispirited and his leg was still swollen. The vet came again and took a blood test which showed that the old horse was fighting an infection.

'Something he got in that mud,' he said. 'It's nasty stuff, that old bog silt. Keep up the Bute and try him with a top feed supplement and keep him turned out unless it gets very wet. Give him time and see what happens.'

'It's a good thing I've got Mack's horse to ride,' Patsy followed the vet out to his car. 'I've been riding him out with some of Rhianne's visitors but Mack will be back soon. I shall miss my old boy for that.'

'So you could use another horse.' The vet looked thoughtful. 'How about a little thoroughbred? It's raced in it's past but it's been used as a trainer's hack for a time now. Trouble is Gethin Jones has put on a bit of weight and he's had to change to riding a cob out to watch his string so it's redundant.'

'It might be a bit sharp for what I need,' Patsy was tempted, and the vet said 'Have a look. He'd probably loan it to you to test it out. I can put in a word for you. I'll leave you his number.'

He scribbled it on his card and drove off and Patsy went back to hug Golly and give him a carrot before turning him out. A new horse to ride was all very well but if Golly never recovered it would be entirely her fault for letting Brian ride him.

Golly wandered off to sniff half-heartedly at the grass and Patsy went rather sadly to clean out her bantams. She knew that she would give in to the temptation to try the horse.

Gethin Jones was quite happy for her to go for a look. The horse was at a small racing yard set below the hills and close to the sea. Gethin. Jones turned out to be a similar age to Patsy, short and stocky and certainly looking more suited to a cob than a race horse but Patsy had googled him and knew that he had been quite a successful trainer in a small way. The yard was modern and well kept and there was a track leading down from it to the beach.

'I don't need much else to gallop them on,' he told Patsy. 'Just a bit of a sandy track round the fields, see. You can give the boy a run round there if you like.'

The boy turned out to be a small, lightly built ex racer, bay with a white streak down his face. He was friendly and when Gethin called a girl to tack him up he was obviously easy to handle. Patsy eyed the light racing saddle doubtfully but the stirrups had long leathers and Geithin said the horse was used to being mounted from the block, unlike most race horses who were used riders vaulting or having a leg up

'Had to teach him this,' Geithin told her when she commented, 'I'm getting beyond all these athletic goings-on now.'

Patsy was relieved. Perhaps the horse would accept another less than agile rider.

As soon as she was on the little horse's back Patsy knew that she would like him. He was not schooled like a riding horse, he went hollow and head high, but he was willing and comfortable and seemed to have no tricks. Patsy cantered him round the sand track and he was happy to have her sitting in the little saddle rather than standing in racing style and he had the light, floating stride of his breed. Patsy pulled beside Gethin smiling and he looked pleased.

'He'd do you fine,' he said. 'You fetch him over and try him for a bit and we'll talk terms. He's done me well, I'll be glad to see him useful again.'

'What is he called?' Patsy asked him.

'"Preseli Lad",' Gethin told her. 'He was bred near here, he's well used to these parts.'

It seemed like an omen and Patsy agreed to the deal.

Katy was envious when Patsy, who had kept quiet about her visit to Gethin, told her about the horse.

'You're having all the fun,' she said resentfully. 'While I just get told to take it easy. It isn't fair.'

'It's perfectly fair,' Patsy decided that it was time to be tough. 'Just be patient for a bit, you've got what you said you wanted, just get on with it.'

'Mum...' Katy started to get angry and then her expression changed and she looked startled, looked down, and put her hand on her stomach. Alarmed Patsy started towards her and then her daughter stared at her, looking utterly amazed.

'It...it moved,' she said. 'I...I felt it move...sort of...fluttering.'

She sat down suddenly on the mounting block and there were tears on her face as she stared at Patsy.

'It...it's real,' she said. 'There really is something... someone...alive in there. I know I saw the scan but...but this, it's incredible. I must tell Gareth.'

She leaped up and ran for their cottage leaving Patsy trying to decide whether to laugh or cry. Her daughter sometimes amazed her.

Patsy had a trek for two visitors next morning which she took out with Osbourne. They were not very experienced but Patsy took them for a slow ride round the flat country at the foot of the hills and home along a quiet bridleway, and it was uneventful apart from her problem of reaching the gate catches from Osbourne's high back. One stiff one proved impossible and she had to dismount to cope with it and then lead the big horse until a bank provided a mounting block. Osbourne looked long suffering and the two ladies with her laughed. Patsy decided that her new acquisition was needed.

She collected Preseli Lad next day and turned him out with Cass who seemed to approve. He left his gate watching and shepherded his new companion off to explore his new field. Watching them Patsy felt mildly intoxicated. The future was starting to look very full of new things.

CHAPTER TWENTY ONE

it was time for the last of the big shows, the Pembrokeshire County. It was a close second to the Royal Welsh, three days of showing and jumping for the equine entries, show classes for cattle, sheep, goats and small animals, exhibition stands for every imaginable form of agriculture and country craft. Once again Hedfa Aur was entered for the in-hand stallion class and Gareth swore that his leg had healed enough for him to show him.

'I've had an idea,' said Katy, when she and Patsy were working on the stallion on the day before the show. 'We've got a name for Cass, what about putting up a notice at the secretary's office asking if anyone knows him? Spotlight can't be a common name for a pony.'

'It's worth a try,' Patsy agreed and Katy went in to set out and print off a photograph of Cass and an appeal for information.

The show might be an echo of the Royal Welsh but the weather was not. It rained all the night before and although it had almost stopped by the time they joined the queue of lorries heading for the show ground it was still grey and windy.

The show was held on the land adjoining the local airfield which meant that it was flat and as it was a permanent site there was enough hard standing for the exhibition stands. The lorry park, however, was not on hard ground and it was already becoming muddy.

'Not good for running,' said Katy, but Gareth said that he would manage. Patsy left them to start getting Hedfa Aur ready and set off down the muddy track to check their entry and put up Katy's notice. There was show jumping under way in one ring and she did not envy the few entries waiting their turn on the slippery grass. There was a horse in now, a rather rough looking black mare, who was making heavy weather of the course. Patsy paused to watch as the set of poles in a spread fence went flying and the rider, a good-looking boy in a flashy light blue show jumping jacket, brought his stick down hard on the horse's flank.

'That horse will be for it later,' said a spectator near Patsy, a girl in riding clothes.

'Yes, Drake's always hard on his horses,' replied her companion. 'Tasty, though, isn't he? '

The first girl laughed. 'Maybe, but down Liz. You'd only be one of the queue.'

They moved off as the commentator announced 'that was twelve faults for Reynard Drake,' and Patsy, feeling sorry for the horse, went on towards the secretary's office in one of the permanent buildings.

By the time that the stallion section of the class for

SOLE POSSESSION

Welsh section D cobs was called it was raining again, the main ring was rapidly becoming churned up, and Patsy could see that Gareth's leg was bothering him. It was Katy who was concerned this time.

'You won't be able to run,' she told him. 'I'll have to do it.'

Predictably Gareth put his foot down and things were starting to get heated when a voice behind them said, 'Problem?' and Mack, dressed for the weather in bright yellow waterproofs, appeared out of the mud and murk and gave Patsy a casual hug.

'Mack,' Patsy, startled, stared at him, 'what are you doing here?'

'I never miss the local festivities,' Mack told her. 'I thought I'd meet up with you here. Just got back from the big outside world last night. Anything I can give a hand with?'

Patsy explained and Mack said, 'I'll have a go if you like. I'm not the best runner but I can try.'

'But do you know what to do?' asked Katy, and Mack said 'It won't be the first time I've been in the ring with this boy, I went in with him right back at his first Cardigan show when he was a foal.'

Patsy remembered it well. Even then Hedfa Aur had shown his quality by winning the foal class while Mack led Eithin Aur with him in the mare and foal class.

Mack proved to have jeans, shirt, and sweater under the yellow outfit, and although his feet were in walking boots, not trainers, it seemed doubtful than anyone would be showing much action in the conditions.

Hedfa Aur was quite used to Mack, having seen and smelled him with his own horse, and he led quite sensibly up to the ring in spite of the rain in his ears. Patsy walked with them hoping to give the horse security and Katy followed, leaving Gareth, looking cross, to rest his leg in the lorry.
The class was quite well filled in spite of the weather. It took more than a bit of rain to put off Welsh cob people. Patsy was slightly alarmed to see the trouble making black among them but today there was a tough looking man handling it and it looked subdued. It was certainly a striking animal, competition for her horse, but Mack coped valiantly with the conditions and Patsy was impressed. Casual riding, chain smoking Mack was far more competent than he appeared, she thought, as he and the sparky cob splashed their way impressively through the trot up.
It took the judge a few minutes of conferring with his plastic wrapped notes and the steward but Hedfa Aur was called in first.
'That was great,' Katy told Mack. 'You looked really professional.'
'I always try to please,' said Mack in a humble voice and Patsy grinned.
Hedfa Aur had to go almost straight back into the ring for the Welsh breed championship and Patsy was thrilled to see Eleri with her lovely mare and Hedfa Aur's daughter in the same class, having won the mare with foal at foot section.
'She's beautiful,' Katy sounded awed, having never seen the foal before. They were all thrilled when

Hedfa Aur was called in as champion and the mare and his daughter were reserve.

Mack came out looking proud and Patsy, taking no notice of Katy's smirk, kissed him. She also congratulated Eleri and admired the foal who was her father in miniature.

'I call that a good day at the office,' said Mack, as they headed back for the lorry, and Katy grinned knowingly at Patsy behind his back.

'Almost worthy of promotion,' she said, and Patsy pretended not to understand.

She had to go back to the secretary's office to sign for her horse's trophies. She was waiting for her turn when she noticed a girl in riding clothes looking at her notice about Cass and something about the way in which she was staring at it caught Patsy's attention. She gave up her place in the short queue and went over.

'Do you recognise the pony?' she asked, and the girl started, looking almost guilty.

'No,' she said sharply. 'I...I mean...I don't think so.'

'Nikki Clarke,' It was the secretary in charge of entries. 'I've got Reynard Drake's slip here...about the complaint.'

'Oh, yes, coming,' the girl backed away from Patsy who was being beckoned to by the trophy secretary and by the time she had signed for Hedfa Aur's beautiful challenge cup the girl had gone, but Patsy remembered the name, the vindictive boy in the show jumping. She hurried back to the box park, she might be able to find him and, probably, the girl called Nikki.

She had definitely looked as if she knew something about the pony, but as Patsy slowed to look round at the parked lorries she had to get out of the way as a smart black Daf drove past, sending mud spattering in all directions. The boy was at the wheel with the girl beside him and Patsy knew that her chance had gone. Back at the lorry Katy was washing the worst of the mud off the stallion with Mack, cigarette in mouth, helping her. Gareth, looking rather disgruntled, was sitting on the lorry step, and as she approached Patsy was glad to see Katy pause in her sponging efforts to give him a hug.

They all admired the cup and Patsy told them about the girl who had been looking at the notice about Cass.

'Shouldn't be hard to trace her,' said Mack. 'You know the jumping boy's name, check him out with the secretary here. Tell you what, I'll do that while you get this lot home.'

Patsy agreed and, saying that he would see her later, Mack went off on his errand.

It had been a tiring day as wet shows always were and successful as it had been Patsy was glad to get home. She was starting on the evening round of feeding everything when Mack drove in.

'Got him,' he told her. 'Address near Pencoed, Cardiff way. I got the impression he isn't too well liked.'

'What next?' wondered Patsy. 'I could try phoning him, but he didn't look the helpful sort.'

'Call on him,' suggested Mack. 'Pick a day when there aren't any big or local shows and you might be lucky.'

SOLE POSSESSION

'Of course it may be a wild goose chase,' said Patsy, but somehow she didn't think so. The girl had looked guilty, although she could not imagine why.

'I'll come with you,' offered Mack. 'Playing sleuth like one of my dashing characters, try it for real.'

'Would you?' Patsy was grateful. She did not much like the thought of tackling the show jumping boy on her own. Mack laughed and hugged her.

'Nothing I'd like better,' he said. 'A day out with good company. Pick a day.'

Patsy said that she would and Mack kissed her.

'Looking forward to it,' he said. 'Now, if I give you a hand here how about coming down to Newport with me for a good reviving meal?'

It certainly sounded more inviting than heating up a frozen dinner and Patsy was tempted but how on earth could she be presentable in time?

'Come as you are,' said Mack cheerfully but Patsy knew that she could not quite do that.

'Half an hour then,' said Mack, as she fed the bantams, and Patsy agreed. After all, it was hardly the Ritz. Realising in surprise that she was going on a date she showered, half-heartedly dried her hair, leaving it damp and fluffy, and put on clean jeans and a fairly dashing blue top. She was ready when she heard Mack's car.

He got out to meet her and looked admiring.

'Transformation,' he said. 'I must say I like that top. Very...er...alluring.'

He was looking quite dashing himself in fawn trousers, a crisp blue denim shirt with long sleeves and a loose cream jacket. His hair was, like hers, still attractively damp and his strong boned face was brown and still youthful. Looking at him Patsy was aware that she might have decisions to make later.

The restaurant was a relaxed family place and Patsy enjoyed the novelty of a meal that she had not thrown together herself. Mack was good company as usual and Patsy knew that she was seeing a different side to him than the casual riding companion or the host parrying his wife's sharp tongue.

The sky had cleared when they came out, there was quite a cool breeze coming off the sea, and Mack walked her the few yards back to his car with his arm round her.

Patsy found that she had made up her mind.

She had wondered if she would still know what to do but in her bed with Mack's long arms round her and his warm, long length against her she found that she remembered very well. Mack went home at dawn, saying that finding him there at breakfast might not be very well received.

'You can break it to Kate later,' he said. 'She'll be prepared next time. There will be a next time?'

'Oh yes, I hope so,' Patsy kissed him. 'Mack...'

'That's alright then,' Mack slid out of bed and almost stepped on the resentful cat who had been banished from her usual spot by Patsy's feet. 'I'll be back later all respectable.'

Katy knew at once of course.

'Did you enjoy your, er, meal then?' she asked, meeting Patsy when she was feeding the horses. 'It must

have taken a long time, it was light when his car left.'
Patsy knew that there was no point in prefabricating. 'Do you mind?' she asked, and Katy looked at her seriously.

'It isn't up to me,' she said. 'But no, I don't mind and I'm not shocked or anything. Do I gather that the tabby cat is out of the picture?'

'Yes,' Patsy turned away from shutting her new horse's door. Mack was coming back to ride later and with a trek next day she wanted give Lad a more ambitious try on the hill. 'They've got a separation.'

'Then good luck,' Katy smiled, putting her hand on her stomach. 'One thing, at your age you haven't got this sort of complication to worry about. He keeps wriggling, very distracting. What on earth will he be like when he's on the loose? I'd better get on, I've work to do this morning. Thank goodness I've stopped feeling sick.'

She went off and Patsy lingered, looking at her other horses in the field. Golly was lying down in the morning sun but he did not look distressed. She had brought Osbourne in ready for Mack but the others were grazing. Patsy leaned on the gate for a minute, pleasantly aware of a gentle languor. It had been good last night, astonishingly good. She was not sure where they would go next but she knew that she was committed to seeing it out.

Preseli Lad looked very light next to Osbourne's solid shape. Mack, already seated on his big horse, looked at him doubtfully as Patsy led him out.

'I hope those fragile little legs are going to be up to

our moors,' he said. 'Give me something with big feet every time.'

'Thoroughbreds are tougher than they look,' Patsy told him hopefully.

She was riding him in Goldie's saddle well-padded out with a sheepskin numnah which she had found in the bottom of the tack box. If all seemed to be going well she would have to buy him a saddle. Gethin had offered to lend her the light saddle in which she had tried him but it was hardly the most inviting thing in which to trek around the hills.

Lad's back sank for a moment when Patsy mounted and she walked him forward quickly to help him adjust. Osbourne followed and by the time they reached the moor gate Lad had accepted the different feel and was walking happily.

They went round Patsy's regular circuit up the side of the old farm and back round the bracken. Lad was light and quick on his feet and although it was not strictly correct his high head carriage and good shoulders made Patsy feel very safe. Cantering felt like flying after kind old Golly's heavy plod and Patsy felt guilty for enjoying it so much at his expense. Back on the flatter ground towards home she could not stop smiling and Mack grinned back.

'That good is he?' he asked, and Patsy laughed.

'Does it show?' she asked, and Mack said 'You look like a kid at Christmas. Come on, let's really go.'

He stood in his stirrups and sent Osbourne forward in his usual casual style and Lad leaped after them. They were soon past the heavier horse, the little thoroughbred light and flying, but as the gate drew closer he was kind and easy to stop and Patsy swung him in a circle to meet the other horse. Mack was laughing as they met and Osbourne dropped back to a trot and he looked suddenly ageless and Patsy had a glimpse of the boy he had once been. "My lover", she thought, the idea striking her with such amazement that she began to laugh as well.

'What?' Mack was smiling, looking at her. 'What's the joke?' but Patsy shook her head.

'Nothing really,' she said. 'Just us, I still find it hard to believe.'

'But you aren't regretting anything?' Mack sounded anxious, and Patsy smiled back.

'No,' she said. 'I just feel a bit…disorientated I suppose. Is it really happening, you and me?'

'I hope so, 'Mack pushed his horse alongside. 'I'd hate to find I'd been dreaming.'

He hung down from the big horse and managed to kiss her.

'I know what you mean,' he said. 'It'll settle, we'll settle, I think we've just found ourselves on a new path, that's all. We have to find our way,' and as they rode on to the gate Patsy knew that they would manage it.

Patsy took Rhianne's visitors out the next day riding Lad and found him ideal, patient when she had to stop to adjust one of her rider's stirrups and sensible when they met wild ponies. He obviously understood what escorting and waiting was all about.

Patsy decided that the coming Monday might be a good time to visit the show jumping boy and Mack agreed. They had spent another night together and this time he had not gone home for breakfast.

It had occurred to Patsy that she might not like her space invaded to this extent but she found it quite natural, waking together, getting dressed with no feeling of embarrassment, and sharing breakfast rituals, tea, toast and cereal for her and two bantam eggs for Mack which he had scrambled for himself. Katy, coming in while they were eating, did give her an embarrassed twinge but Mack seemed completely undisturbed even at Katy's slight innuendo when she greeted him with 'Hi Mack, sleep well?'

'Yes thank you Kate,' he said blandly, looking her in the eye, and Katy clearly thought better than to say any more.

Mack had offered to drive and certainly he had the better car, a sleek silver BMW, and in spite of the reason for the journey Patsy felt a sensation of freedom as they swung onto the motorway. For a few hours she had no animals or trekkers to think about and no family to suddenly present any problems.

Patsy realised that she had never before been on more than a local trip in a car driven by Mack. The car was smooth and fast and Mack, whom she had been afraid might drive as he rode, proved to be an excellent driver, slipping the car along right on the speed limit and overtaking with no fuss or risks. There was simple, popular classical music on the radio and Patsy relaxed. It might not quite be a carefree day out but it felt like one. They talked as they always had about anything and everything, the journey, horses, world news, and, more recent, themselves, their feelings and the future.

'I'd like you to consider us living together,' Mack told her. 'But I know you wouldn't want to leave Bryn Uchaf and all your commitments to move in with me. I could let my house but I don't want you to feel bound to take me in.'

'Like a lost cat,' Patsy laughed. 'I wouldn't feel like that at all, I think it's what I want too, but perhaps we should just go on as we are for a bit and let things happen. I really have got feelings for you Mack, in every way, but we've both been here before. I don't want to waste time but we need to be sure.'

'I am,' said Mack softly, 'but you're right. Stupid to rush. But don't let's leave it too long, time does move very fast. I'd hate to find it was too late.'

'Mack...' Patsy, looking at him, felt a pang at the thought of that time passing, and realised that, however she might try to avoid admitting it, she actually was coming to love him. She really would not leave it long to work out what came next.

The show jumper's address, when they found it some time later, did not look promising. It was an ordinary semi-detached house with a small garden and no sign of horses. The door, when they rang the bell, was answered by a middle-aged lady wearing navy blue trousers and a plain blue sweater who said that it was her son they wanted.

'He's at the stables,' she told them 'although it's horses he's got, not ponies.'

It sounded hopeful, and they followed her instructions for a few miles until a turning took them to under a motorway bridge and to a sign reading Laurel Stables.

It turned out to be a small DIY yard, a two-sided block of stable round a rather messy yard with a field behind. There was a sand school in which the boy from the show was riding the black mare that they had seen at the show with the girl adjusting a high set of upright rails. The girl saw them at once and Patsy saw her startled reaction.

The boy was riding the horse at the jump, bringing his stick down hard as she hesitated, and she made a panicky leap, bringing the poles crashing down, and getting another smack as she landed.

'Put it up again,' shouted the boy. 'And bring those stands closer, jam those poles in so that she learns that hitting them hurts.'

'Drake...' called the girl.'wait.'

'What..?' he looked round, saw Patsy and Mack, and pulled his horse up.

'If you're looking for Mrs. Elliot she isn't here,' he told them, and Mack said 'You'll do. We're just after some information.'

Looking impatient the boy turned his horse across the school towards them. He was good looking, Patsy saw, dark and very confident with blue eyes and muscular arms, but he also looked hard and arrogant.

'What is it then?' he demanded, and Patsy said 'we're trying to find the owner of a pony which seems to have been abandoned.'

'So why does that affect me?' the boy looked cross. 'I

haven't lost any ponies.'

'Drake,' the girl sounded hesitant. 'I think it might be Sylva's pony. There...there was a notice about it at the show.'

'Oh,' for a moment the boy looked down, then he stared at them 'But why come asking me? It's Marg they should be asking.'

'And who is Marg?' Mack asked him, and Nikki said, 'she's got a yard a few miles away, Berry Farm. There was a pony there like the one on the notice, and...and Syl used to call it Spot.'

'Spotlight,' Drake sounded scornful. 'Because her mother is on the stage or something.'

'And he had those white bits,' Nikki told them. 'She...she had an accident, I think they blamed the pony.'

'And us,' said Drake crossly. 'Because we wouldn't let her ride with us or something. I don't see why it was our fault it bolted.'

'Did someone hit it?' Patsy had an inkling of what might have happened. It had been the threat of being hit that had sent Cass off with Katy.

'Only the kid on it,' Drake dug his heels into his horse and swung her away. 'Come on Nikki, get this jump up again.'

'Where is Berry Farm?' Patsy asked Nikki, and she said 'turn left out of here, next on the right, about two miles down. Tell Marg we're really sorry about Syl. Alright Drake, I'm coming.'

Back in the car Patsy and Mack looked at each other.

'I think your mystery is almost solved,' said Mack. 'It's

a shame it wasn't that boy who had the accident.'

'I can see why Nikki didn't want to admit at the show that she knew something,' Patsy told him.

'She seemed too nice a kid to be mixed up with a nasty bit of work like him.'

'She'll learn,' said Mack. 'Come on, let's find the end of this trail.'

Berry Farm turned out to be another DIY yard but a better cared for one than Laurel Stables and when Patsy explained why they had come Marg looked delighted.

'Is he alright?' she asked. 'Abandoned? That man was supposed to run a sanctuary. I did wonder, but Sylva's mother gave me no choice. Oh, come on in, I'll make coffee and we'll sort this out.'

Inside Marg's big, untidy kitchen she made coffee and produced short bread and Patsy told her the whole story and Marg told them her part in it.

'I shouldn't have let that women persuade me to get rid of him,' she said. 'There had to be an explanation, Spot was always terrified of sticks from the time when Syl got him. She'd surely not have hit him herself, unless...unless that boy said something that really upset her. She was getting obsessed with him, he led her on, thought it was funny when she was such an odd little thing.'

'And she's still in a coma?' asked Patsy. 'But it must be months...'

'Yes,' Marg looked sad. 'I know they've almost given up hope, only Simon, her brother, still insists she'll come out of it. They're twins, you know, very close,

almost telepathic, at least until Drake came along.'
"Telepathic" Patsy remembered the bay pony, running alone in the moonlight, almost as if someone was riding him, and the music...
'Did she ever ride him to music?' she asked, and Marg laughed.
'Dressage to music,' she said. 'She had a passion for it, something about the whole process, the music, the rhythm, the way she and the pony almost became one with it, it was magical to watch.
If you like I've got a video.'
'We'd love to see it,' Patsy told her and Marg found the disc and switched on the player.
'This was at the British Dressage to music championships,' she told them. 'Sylva won her class, novice, but brilliant.'
The screen showed Spotlight, plaited and polished, a brow band set with crystals on his bridle, waiting to enter a floodlit indoor arena. His rider was a slight girl with blond hair restrained in a sparkling net at the back of her neck below her riding hat. She wore a fitted, full skirted black show jacket with shiny buttons, a satin stock with sparkling silver threads, white breeches and shining black boots. Her hands were in white gloves above the striking white patch on her pony's neck, and Patsy again remembered the weird effect of white hands in the moonlight.
'Her wretched mother spent a small fortune dressing her,' said Marg wryly. 'It's a shame she couldn't think beyond the gloss.'
Sylva raised her arm to signal that she was ready to

start and a run of warning chords took her into the arena and to a first halt before the music, an arrangement of 'Greensleeves,' took them forward at trot.

It was a riveting display, the music, completely suiting the pony's type and way of going, all had a feel of folk music and tradition. It fitted perfectly to the changing paces, trot, canter, walk, changes of rein and shortening and lengthening stride. There was a suggestion of counter-canter, varying circles, and a striding free walk. Rider and pony looked engrossed, away in a world of their own, expressing the music in their own style, until a final jaunty theme took them down the centre line to a balanced halt facing the judges, perfectly in time with the music. Patsy found that she had been mesmerised herself, and Mack said 'What a beautiful thing.'

It expressed the effect perfectly, it had been a thing, something complete in itself, and Marg sighed as she switched off the player.

'Yes,' she said. 'They should have gone on, an understanding like that could have taken them anywhere, in spite of the pony limitations. But perhaps now they might get a second chance, if Sylva recovers.'

'What do you think we should do now?' Patsy asked her. 'I'm happy to keep the pony officially, if her mother agrees, and he'd still be there if she needs him.'

'I think you'll find she just wants it to stay lost,' Marg told her. 'She won't really accept what happened to Syl, the girl was always a bit of an embarrassment to her, being a bit different. She's an actress, you see, plays a saintly mother in one of the soaps. An odd, wayward child she finds it hard to communicate with would be bad for her image although she'd have accepted a showy successful riding one.'

'What about the brother?' asked Mack. 'You said they were close.'

'Yes,' Marg nodded. 'He may only be seventeen but he's very responsible and he's been trying to trace the pony. I'll phone him now, he may be at the hospital as it's school holiday time.'

She was right, Simon was on the veranda which ran along Syl's side of the building, trying to think of something that might bring Syl back. She was very close, the doctor said, but he still thought that her waking brain was refusing to let her face something. Marg's news gave him instant hope.

'The pony,' he said. 'If she could actually touch it. If I can arrange something would these people bring him here?'

'Yes,' said Patsy at once, when Marg relayed the request. 'Tell him to talk to the hospital and 'phone me.' Simon agreed to do his best, and Marg, looking pleased, shut her 'phone.

'I do hope it works,' she told Patsy and Mack. 'I've felt bad about the whole thing for so long.'

Driving home Patsy was hoping the same.

'It was so beautiful,' she said to Mack. 'I must borrow that disk to show Katy. We have to get them together again.'

'It may never be possible,' Mack warned her soberly. 'A coma for this long, there's no certainty she'll ever really recover.'

CHAPTER TWENTY TWO

Sylva's doctor and the hospital authorities agreed to the experiment. Sylva's bed could be moved onto the veranda, a solid brick construction meant as an outdoor place for patients who needed fresh air, and the pony could be led round to it.

'I'll come with you,' declared Katy, when she heard. 'I've got to know Cass, Spot, pretty well, he's even thought I'm his owner. I must be there to see what happens when they meet.'

'It may not work,' Patsy warned her, but although Mack would have been happy to go with her Patsy knew that it was Katy's prerogative.

Cass was quite happy to load into the lorry and they set off on a calm green and blue day with the trees at their heaviest and the roads busy with tourists. A space had been marked off for them in a corner of the car park and the pony clattered down the ramp and stared about. A tall, fair haired boy was waiting for them and introduced himself as Sylva's brother. He patted the pony and when Cass pricked his ears he smiled.

'Oh yes,' he said. 'It really is Spotlight. I told Syl that he was coming to see her but I don't know if she could hear.'

They followed him round the side of the building, Katy leading the pony, Patsy walking behind. She was feeling nervous, it would be such an anti-climax if this did not work.

There was a hospital bed out on the veranda, a stand with drips beside it and a heart monitor. The figure propped up a little under the sheet looked young and slight and her blond hair, cut short, was the same colour as Katy's. Cass followed Katy a little hesitantly up the slope and under the overhanging roof, his shoes clattering on the hard surface, and Simon, at the bedside, took his sister's hand. A nurse and doctor hovered watchfully in the background.

'Syl,' he said. 'Your pony's here, Spot, he's looking for you.'

Katy led Cass up to the bed, the pony snorting a bit, and staring, but then he reached out his head to sniff and his ears went forward. He was pushing his nose into her limp arm as he had to Katy and for a tense moment there was no reaction. Then Sylva's arm moved, her hand went up to fondle the warm, questing nose, and her eyes opened, and focussed.

'Spot,' she said. 'Oh Spot, I didn't mean to hit you...they laughed...oh Spot, I'm sorry.'

She was stroking his nose, tears running down her face, and the pony blew a warm breath over her, nuzzling into her neck, then Syl looked round, suddenly looking alarmed, and the doctor said 'Reassure her

Simon, she doesn't know where she is.'

'Syl,' Simon was holding her other hand. 'It's alright Syl, you knocked your head falling off. You knocked yourself out for a bit.'

"Understatement of the year," thought Patsy, who found that she had tears in her own eyes. The girl was looking round, confused, clinging to the pony's forelock with one hand and her brother's hand with the other and the nurse came forward reassuringly and checked the blood pressure monitor attached to her arm.

'Just stay with her for a bit,' advised the doctor. 'Keep talking to her and keep that animal close. It can eat some of the grass out there when she feels confident to let it move away.'

Gradually, with Simon quietly telling his sister where she was and that her pony had been well cared for, Syl's clinging hands relaxed and her eyes closed. Checking again the nurse assured them that she was alright.

'She's just sleeping,' she told them. 'Her brain needs to relax, let the surprise of coming round sink in.'

Simon stayed with his sister while Katy took Spot to graze on the short hospital turf a few feet away. Patsy found a bench from which to watch and she and Katy took it in turns to hold the pony. Syl woke several times and they took the pony back to her. Patsy went in search of the hospital shop and the drinks machine and kept them supplied, but they could not stay forever. In the end Simon promised Syl that her pony would come back next day and Patsy drove him to

Marg's stables.

She was delighted to hear what had happened and readily agreed to keep the pony and take him back to the hospital next day.

'He can stay here as long as he needs,' she said. 'Until Syl's future is sorted out.'

'And I'll have him back if I'm needed,' Patsy promised.

She and Katy drove home through the warm evening, feeling a quiet satisfaction. In the field Lad, missing his friend, whinnied as they drove in but Golly, who would normally have greeted them as well, remained where he was, lying down again. Some of Patsy's satisfaction faded. If only she could find a way to help him as well.

Mack was delighted to hear that the trip had been a success. Lying beside him that night, their hands joined and the cat reclaiming her spot by her feet, Patsy said 'I wonder if there really was some sort of telepathy between Syl and the pony. There's certainly something between them, he knew her straight away, even in that bed, although it seems impossible.'

'Why?' Mack asked her. 'There is something intangible in the way horses think, they have their own wavelengths, and a trauma like the one those two shared could have made some connection.'

'Like tuning a radio,' Patsy agreed. 'I'm just so glad I found Cass...Spotlight, for her.'

'Fate,' Mack turned towards her. 'Things work out if you let them, as I hope they will for us.'

'I think they will,' Patsy saw the depth of warmth in his eyes and pulled his head down to kiss him. 'I really think they will.'

There was good news from Simon in the next few days. Sylva was improving and Marg had brought Spot over to graze near her each day.

'She'll have to go in a rehabilitation unit for a time,' he told Patsy. 'But there's a place she can go where they can accommodate the pony. Our mother's had to accept having him back, she admits she was wrong to make Marg get rid of him.'

'It's great news,' Patsy told Katy and Mack. 'But of course Aled Williams is going to get away with that sanctuary scam of his. I wonder how many more ponies he's dumped.'

It was only the following day that they learned about more. Patsy had taken a slow trek round the flat moor in the morning but Lad had felt fresh and she and Mack took their horses for a gallop, heading for home as the gradually shortening day turned to dusk. As they rode down the hill Mack said 'look,' and Patsy saw the figure on foot with a horse opening the moor gate and the shadowy shape of the lorry parked nearer the road.

'He's at it again,' exclaimed Patsy. 'We'll never get there in time to challenge him.'

'No, but it looks as if he's got another problem,' said Mack, and Patsy saw the led horse spin round, almost pulling the man at its head over, as the grey stallion burst through the bushes near him, shrieking a challenge.

'I reckon that's a colt he's trying to dump,' said Mack as the led horse reared. The man was trying to remove its halter but he was knocked off his feet as the grey stallion waded in and the newcomer turned to run. With the intruder routed the stallion swung back to drive his mare's away from the threat, the other horse was out of the gate back to the road, and the man, a half visible shape in the thickening dusk, remained on the ground.

'Looks as though he's got more than he bargained for,' said Mack.'we'd better get down there.'

He sent Osbourne on down the hill and Patsy let her excited little horse follow. The loose horse was away towards the road and Patsy hoped that it would not meet a car.

Aled Williams was sitting up when they reached him, clutching an arm. Mack dropped off Osbourne handed his reins to Patsy and went to him.

'It looks as though you got your comeuppance for that game,' he told the man. 'What is it? More donations for your sanctuary?'

'I don't know what it is you're talking about,' Aled Williams sounded shaky but defensive. 'Just doing a friend a favour I was. Got a broken arm for my trouble.'

'Shame,' said Mack ironically. 'You'll have problems driving that heap home with that, won't you?'

'You'll not be after leaving me here like this.' He let his arm go to use the other hand to get up and dropped back, swearing.

'What do I do with him?' Mack appealed to Patsy, who said 'he could stay here till morning, it's not cold.'

'Unless he swears to give up his "sanctuary",' said

Mack, and Aled said 'I'll not be doing this again,
I tell you. Just get me sorted can't you?'
'I suppose we have to help him,' said Patsy. 'I'll phone Katy, Gareth might come and take him over the hill to A and E.'
'While we see where the horse has got to,' said Mack.
Gareth came and Mack helped Aled Williams to his car. He looked sick and white in the light inside and Mack took pity on him enough to make a support for the arm with a spare sweater of Gareth's.
Aled Williams was worrying about his lorry and Mack said that he would collect it later and park it at Bryn Uchaf until he recovered.
They drove off and Patsy said, 'How on earth do we find the horse?'
'I don't think it'll be too hard,' said Mack, and he was right. They were at the top of the Bryn Uchaf drive when there was a rapid thud of un-shod hooves behind them and the colt came pushing up. Katy was watching for them and when she spotted the extra horse she opened the gate so that it was not tempted to try to cross the cattle grid and it crowded in behind them with Lad and Osbourne flattening their ears at it. In the field Hedfa Aur scented it and came to his gate shrieking a challenge and the colt cowered, hiding behind the two ridden horses.
'Keep out of its way Kate, I'll deal with it.' Mack dismounted and Katy took his horse while he got some nuts in a bowl and held them out. The colt dived at them and Mack moved sharply back into the stable, opening a door, and as soon as the colt was in he

dropped the bowl and came quickly out.
'It seems we return one and get a repeat performance with another,' he said, as he took Osbourne from Katy. 'That was a slick bit of movement,' Katy sounded impressed, and Mack said 'Monty Roberts is my second name. A bit of food usually works.'
The colt was skewbald, about thirteen hands, rough and clumsily built, and there was a mark round his neck that looked as if it had been made with a tether strap.
'It'll have to stay there for the night,' said Patsy. 'We'll sort something out in the morning.'
'How much would a bet be worth that it's here for a lot longer than that,' said Mack.
The colt looked no more impressive in daylight and he was very nervous but when Katy stayed talking to him he gradually gained confidence enough to come closer and sniff her hands and let her scratch his neck. 'I think he's quite a kind little thing,' she told Patsy, turning away and stroking the by now distinct bulge at her waist. 'We'll need a pony one day for this one.'
Patsy laughed. 'Quite a lot of days,' she said. 'But he looks as if he'll be old enough to break next year. He might make a trekking pony. I don't see him going anywhere in any case. We'll have to talk Gareth and Mack into making a decent enclosure for him until I can get him gelded.'
Katy grinned. 'I don't think talking Mack into anything for you will be hard,' she said. 'You really are turning into quite an item.'
'Yes,' Patsy considered it thoughtfully. It was true,

being with Mack seemed already an established thing. Katy was looking at her seriously.

'Are you comfortable with it?' she asked. 'I mean...after the way things went with Dad. I know you once said, when he got so difficult, never again.'

'I know,' Patsy remembered. 'But I really think this is different.'

She hoped it was true, but she knew that she would soon have to decide how deeply she could let their commitment go.

Gareth and Mack cheerfully agreed to building a fence and Patsy got the vet to check the pony over.

'He's a three year old,' he told her. 'Typical traveller's pony. You'll never trace the owner. Nothing wrong with it that a bit of decent food won't cure. I'll back you over a passport if you go for one.'

Patsy thanked him and asked him to have another look at Golly, who was lying down again in his box. The vet shook his head.

'He's just not been able to shake off that infection, whatever it was,' he said. 'I don't want to keep pumping antibiotics into him. I'll give him a vitamin pick me up, but he's at an age when some of them don't climb back.'

He gave the old horse an injection and Golly, now on his feet, sniffed half-heartedly at Patsy's pocket and the vet patted him. 'Don't give him up yet,' he said. 'Just look after him.'

He drove off and Patsy put Golly back into his stable. It was hot again and the flies were annoying the horses in the field. Goliath could stay in out of their way.

Mack and Gareth completed the enclosure and Patsy found a head collar to fit the colt and discovered that he was halter broken enough to lead out to it. Hedfa Aur shouted his objection to a possible rival but the colt ignored him. The grass was good and he tore into it in a way that showed he had not seen anything like it for some time.

Mack went home to work, saying that it was time he rescued his hero from the predicament in which he had left him

'There's talk of a television airing for him and his doings,' he said. 'It would be a nice bit extra towards me buying out Tab's share of the house.'

'Is that what you hope to do?' Patsy asked him, and he said that it was.

'My agreeing to do that is part of the separation agreement,' he said. 'If we work things out and I
don't want to live in it I can always let it.'

'Mack...' Patsy still hesitated and Mack squeezed her shoulder.

'No rush,' he said. 'Whatever you decide, so long as it somehow includes me.'

He went without waiting for an answer and Patsy was left thoughtful. Looking round her kitchen with her own things around and her own routines to follow, she imagined changing, the constant signs and feeling of another person in residence, the hint of male presence in the scent of aftershave and healthy male sweat, the whiff of cigarette smoke and the loss of complete privacy. In contrast she remembered cold,

dark days, Katy and Gareth with their separate lives, the cats and the television for company, and no warm smile when she entered a room, no comfortable talk and warm
loving nights, no support in emergencies, practical or emotional, and she thought that perhaps she did know what she wanted.

Gareth and Patsy went into their cottage to work and Patsy ate a sandwich and did some half-hearted cleaning and went back outside. The shadows were lengthening and as she leaned on the gate watching the horses she saw a white shape rise above the trees which went down to the stream. It was the egret, flying straight and true, both wings spread and strong again, its legs stretched out behind in the way of all the heron family. Suddenly Patsy knew what to do about another of her problems.

Golly was on his feet in the stable and Patsy fastened on his head collar. He was stiff after his time in but he followed carefully as she led him down the stony path into the wood and down to the stream.

It was very quiet down there, just the sound of the water singing as it went over the stony bed. The trees were still, their leaves heavy with the last of summer, and the banks of the stream were lush with grass and ferns. Golly followed her carefully into the water, lowering his head to sniff and drink, and Pasty led him slowly down stream to the pool below the bluestone rocks. There she stopped and perched on a rock close to the bank while Golly stood relaxed, his ears first pricking then relaxing. The water was very clear,

Patsy could see surprised little fish swerving round their feet, and the otter briefly appeared before diving out of sight under the far bank. She lost all sense of time, the shadows deepened under the trees and she and the old horse stayed still, held there by the sense of a presence before and beyond any man-made time. It was almost dark when she roused, the spell broken by the sharp cry of an owl landing in a tree close by. Golly raised his head, snorting, and Patsy realised that her feet were cold and her bottom numb from the rocky seat. It was time to go back.

Golly turned to go with her and it seemed to Patsy that he was not quite so stiff. They made their way back along the water to the slope out and up the path towards the house, the darkness almost complete, just a gleam along the western horizon, and Patsy saw the figure waiting for her at the gate.

'Mack,' she said, as he opened the gate and put his arms round her. 'How did you know where I'd gone?'

'The horses showed me,' Mack told her. 'They were all at this end of their fields, keeping a look out.

Tabs, she always said there was a power down there. Did you find it?'

'I don't know,' Patsy leaned her head on his shoulder. 'Something happened. Oh Mack, I'm so tired. I feel as though I've been away, somewhere, for ages.'

'Come on,' Mack kissed her. 'Golly can go back in his field and you can come in. I'm here, I'll look after you.' Golly went quite freely away to join the others and Patsy let Mack lead her home. To their home, she thought sleepily. What other future did she want?

CHAPTER TWENTY THREE.

Six weeks later two riders cantered their horses up the side of the Hafod fields. Autumn had touched the bracken with brown and scarlet berries were bright on the rowan tree at the corner. The air had been sharp that morning with the first touch of frost. Most of the sheep had gone to winter grazing and the grey stallion had taken his mares and their rapidly growing foals to the more sheltered lowlands. The horses slowed to a walk as they reached the top and Patsy patted Golly's damp neck. Mack grinned at her.

'Getting back to normal I see,' he said, and Patsy agreed.

'He's been getting there ever since our visit to the ancients,' she said. 'It was so strange, Mack, the feeling of something going through us, using local energy. I've wondered if I imagined it, but look at the change in him. The vet had almost written him off.'

'"There are more things..."', quoted Mack. 'Hamlet was right there. Just accept it and feel thankful.'

'I do,' Patsy told him. 'For many things. Katy's baby coming, Sylva and her pony together again and...

and us, you and me.'

'Yes,' said Mack quietly. 'I'll second that.'

He reached over from Osbourne's back to squeeze her hand and they smiled at each other. This was the best of all those things, thought Patsy.

The end.

Printed in Great Britain
by Amazon